Rusty Wilson's

Favorite
Bigfoot
Campfire
Stories

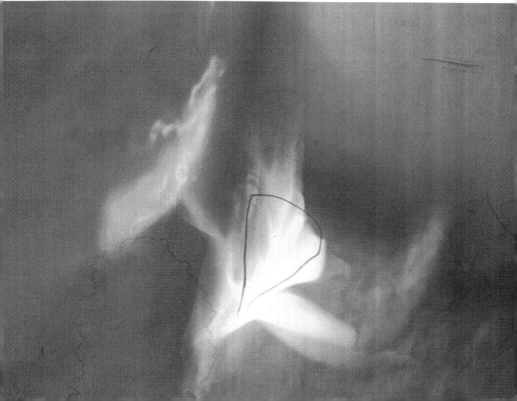

I think those who are fortunate enough to see Bigfoot may not realize their good luck, but they are truly blessed to have had a connection with another species that may be as smart as humans, even if it did scare the pants off them. —Rusty Wilson

· FOR ·

Maya

Contents

Foreword

· ·

by Rusty Wilson

Greetings, fellow adventurers, to this set of nineteen Bigfoot campfire stories, stories guaranteed to either make you smile or scare the socks off you. I've put this collection together for those of you who enjoy the craziness and scariness of Bigfootery and are ready for more hijinks.

This book is a compilation of three of my ebooks: *Ten Tense Bigfoot Campfire Stories, Six Short Bigfoot Campfire Stories*, and *Rusty Wilson's Hairy Trio of Bigfoot Campfire Stories*. I've combined them into a book for those of you who don't have ebook readers or for those who just want to have them in print. These stories are also some of my favorites.

These stories were collected around many campfires, where my flyfishing clients regaled and scared me to death with their Bigfoot encounters. I think those who are fortunate enough to see Bigfoot may not realize their good luck, but they are truly blessed to have had a connection with another species that may be as smart as humans, even if it scared the pants off them.

So, pull up a chair or log, kick back with some hot chocolate, and be prepared to read some tales that will make your hair stand on end—or maybe make you wonder if you might like to meet the Big Guy himself.

[1] Tree Snags and Wood Knockers

. . . .

I was guiding a flyfishing trip up the North Fork of the White River near Meeker, Colorado, when I heard this story from a local guy. It was quite the tale, and he told it with a lot of feeling, keeping us all on the edges of our seats, or in this case, logs. Since we were close to the area he was telling about, it was quite personal, and I don't think any of us got much sleep that night.

Of course, it didn't help much that my cook went out and did some wood-knocking during the night to help the mood, which he admitted to the next morning. What was really memorable, though, was that he was mad because someone had pulled his tent along a few feet during the night. He figured they were getting even with him for the wood-knocking. When no one would admit to it (and it was a pretty straightforward bunch), and he realized how difficult a feat it would be, he got a little white. I'll never forget that, and I'll never forget the following story.
—Rusty

When we were in our early twenties, my friend Rowdy and I went on somewhat of a backpacking binge. We had grown up together in the same neighborhood, a redneck area in

Meeker, Colorado, and we'd learned to hunt and fish and do everything a good Western Colorado boy learned in those days, so we were pretty adept at taking care of ourselves.

I say in those days because this was some twenty years ago, and we both grew up and went on to bigger things, although I can't necessarily say better. Rowdy's now a pilot for a major airlines, and I started a company that makes safety gear for miners.

This incident I'm about to relate was what triggered us to get out of town and make something of ourselves, if you want to call it that. It definitely put an end to our backpacking.

Rowdy and I had one thing in common—we both loved the outdoors. And I don't mean in a sense that would make one want to become a nature writer or photographer, but more in the sense that we wanted to be wild men and never be indoors again in our lives, but instead go live in caves and explore and eat berries and all that. It was the freedom.

Of course, it was a romantic notion, based on watching TV shows about people like Grizzly Adams and reading about the old-time trappers. Actually, now that I think of it, we were both kind of rebels, and the wilderness represented an escape from convention and society for us.

In any case, neither of us amounted to much by society's standards. Rowdy worked at the local gas station and I did janitorial work when I could get it. It was amazing we'd both even managed to graduate high school. I know Rowdy was kicked out several times for smoking on the school grounds, and I had my share of problems, too.

But we now lived for the times we could get out, and Rowdy finally bought an old beater pickup, which represented a major turn in things for us, as it meant we could finally get out and away.

It was early summer when he bought the truck, and we both immediately quit our jobs. We planned on spending the entire summer exploring and backpacking.

We'd both managed to save a little money, and we figured we could pull it off, then come back to civilization and get jobs again in the fall—unless, by some luck, we figured out a way to just live out there in the wilds permanently. I think our parents were hoping for the latter by this time, as they'd pretty much had it with us.

We had a great time that summer, exploring all over the place and coming into town to resupply and say hello to our parents so they wouldn't worry too much. The memories we created during that short summer have stuck with me all my life, and I know they're pretty special for Rowdy, too. We basically just went feral and lived like wild men.

We had our health and our youth and our wild ideas and it all went together into a very special time, living out there in our little backpacking tents, hiking all over and finding things we had no idea even existed—or things we had no idea existed finding us, I should say.

It was late September, and we'd just come back up into the high country from town, our packs topped out with fresh supplies. We knew it might be our last trip out, as it looked to be an early winter, with fresh snow already hitting the high country, though it had melted.

All the outfitters were talking about how business was down, as people were thinking it was going to be a short autumn, and all the deer and elk would be hightailing it into the low country, far from the hunters. Rowdy and I knew this because my uncle was an outfitter (Lone Joe Outfitting, North Fork of the White River).

When he found out we were going out backpacking again, he warned us to get back within a week, as there was a storm brewing in the Arctic that looked like it was going to come down our way. He watched the weather more than most weathermen, and he'd also seen all the signs of an early and hard winter.

He grew up in the backcountry, and I trusted his knowledge, so for Rowdy and me, it was kind of a poignant time, as we knew it would probably be our last trip—which it was, but not for the reason we thought it would be.

We were determined to go out with a bang, though, and planned our last outing as a seven-day backpacking trip across the Flattop Mountains, not far from Meeker. My uncle told us we were nuts, as these mountains are pretty high in elevation, and he knew it was already freezing up there.

But Rowdy and I were seasoned mountain men by then, so we thought. Actually, I don't know what we were thinking—maybe that if we got snowed in we'd just end up like the old trappers, sitting around some big fire inside a make-do teepee with some good-looking Indian girls—or something like that. Youth just doesn't know how to worry properly, I guess, and kids like us hadn't had the chance yet to find out all the things that can go wrong.

We were going to start at Trapper's Lake, a beautiful large alpine lake right in the heart of the Flattops, then pretty much hike straight across to the little town of Yampa, which set on the other side of the mountains.

Of course, there were a number of rugged peaks and cliffs that would prevent a straight line traverse, and we knew this, so my uncle had helped us plan out a trek that would take us up and through a number of drainages.

The Flattops are named that for a reason—they're huge mesas capped with volcanic basalts which give them their flat tops and also create huge cliffs that ring the tops, making it hard to get through them.

So, we stuffed our packs to the gills and headed out, parking the truck at the Trapper's Lake Lodge. The owners there knew my uncle well. We would hitch a ride back once we came out on the Yampa side. That was the plan, anyway. It was a good forty miles or more, quite a hike, but we were young and strong and fearless and maybe a bit in denial, which is nicer than saying we were dumb.

Oh man, the first few miles carrying a big pack always eats a man alive. After awhile, you get your second wind and it slacks off, but the start is always hard. It takes awhile for your blood to get oxygenated. But at first, it was easy flat going as we circled the lake, and we met a few people there who would all say hello and want to know where we were going.

But one fellow we met on the trail left a bad taste in my mouth. He kind of took the wind out of my sails, though he didn't seem to bother Rowdy any.

He was just a regular-looking sort of fellow, maybe in his forties, kind of shaggy with a short beard and longish hair, wearing a small pack and looking like he'd been out enough to know how to take care of himself. When we met him on the trail, he didn't even bother to say hello, he just stopped and started kind of lecturing us with concern.

"Look, boys," he said. "You be real careful out there. As you probably know, there's been some big fires up here in the last few years, and you're going to be hiking through a lot of snags, you know, standing dead trees. They're very dangerous, and it takes almost nothing to knock one down. I had a couple almost come down on top of me out on the trail just today. Try not to put your tents anywhere near them, as a night breeze will push them down right on top of you."

We thanked him for his advice and started back up the trail, but he wasn't done. It's what he said next that left me feeling unsettled.

"And when you hear the Wood Knockers, get the hell out. You're going smack into their territory, and you wouldn't be the first ones to just disappear out there. Trust me on this one, kids."

I stopped and turned, watching the hiker start back down the trail, seeming intent on making good time out. I just stood there for awhile, wondering what he'd meant. Finally, Rowdy kind of hit my shoulder, saying "C'mon, let's get going," but I just stood there. I felt weird all of a sudden, the first time ever in my life I questioned what I was doing.

Rowdy said, "Wood Knockers are just a myth. If they existed, we would've seen them by now cause we've been living in their supposed territory all summer. C'mon, don't let him scare you, let's go. He's full of it."

We continued on up the trail, but I was now more wary. Wood Knockers—Bigfoot. There had been rumors of them in the Flattops for years. In fact, I remembered a story my uncle told about being out with some hunting clients sitting around a campfire and hearing the most ungodly scream that went on and on all night. After that, my uncle wouldn't go alone out in the mountains, even though he'd never seen anything remotely like a Bigfoot.

He also knew some people who had come up on the other side of the mountains, over by Deep Creek, and found a weird assortment of clothes tossed around along the creek. As they were standing there trying to figure it out, they saw a huge dark figure come from the thick forest and just stand there, and they left immediately.

These were the stories I conveniently forgot when back-packing with Rowdy—until meeting the hiker, that was. But we hadn't been in the Flattops until now. Suddenly my pack felt even heavier than before. I kind of thought for a moment about my mom's good crockpot stew and wondered if she'd made any lately. I hadn't thought about anything homey since we'd started our wild man lifestyle that spring.

We carried on, right on up the trail and up the mountain. I swear, this was our last trip in and should've been the easiest because I was in top shape after a summer of backpacking, but it seemed harder and harder, the further we got. I finally mentioned it to Rowdy.

He answered, "It's just cause you're feeling uncertain from what that hippie-looking dude told you, that's all. You have to rekindle the charge."

I didn't say much and just followed Rowdy on upwards. I was thinking that a big crate of dynamite would be about the right charge to get me rekindled. Not much else would have any effect.

We found a nice place to camp that night, in a beautiful clearing by a little pond, surrounded by old narrow-leaf cottonwood trees, nary a snag in sight. I was so tired I slept like a rock, if rocks can sleep, and Bigfoot never crossed my mind.

The next day I was re-energized, and so was Rowdy. Our old enthusiasm was back, and we made good time, hiking up a long drainage and finding a way up onto the top of a huge mesa. The views were awesome. We decided to try and make good time and get back down on the other side before dark, which we managed to do with a lot of effort. We both slept like babies that night, forgetting all about Wood Knockers.

The next day, our third day in, we climbed up another drainage, which was tough going, as there weren't many animal trails, and we had to fight our way through scrub-oak underbrush.

When we got on top, we could see what looked to be the leading edge of a storm way out far to the west, and I can't say this made either of us very happy. We were now in the heart of the Flattops Wilderness. Our mountain man romanticism was quickly settling into the reality of pure physical survival in the high mountains. We were at 10,000 feet.

Once again, we made good time. Unlike our previous trips, we both now felt a sense of urgency, and I could tell the barometric pressure was dropping. I'd been out enough to recognize how the dropping pressure affected me, and this felt like a big one coming in. Why we didn't just turn around when we saw the storm coming in I'll never know.

The next day, our fourth, we woke to overcast skies and a sense of foreboding. Gray tendrils of clouds melted around the mountain tops above us.

We broke camp with an even greater sense of urgency. It really felt like snow was coming—there was that cold clamminess to the air that usually preceded a big snowfall, and the air smelled different, like it always does before a big storm.

We packed up again, took a few minutes to study our topo maps, then headed out. We needed to make good time, as we had many miles to go before we were even vaguely near civilization. I was beginning to wish I'd listened to my uncle.

The day wore on as we slogged along. Finally, it was getting late, so we started looking for a place to set up camp. Just like the hiker had said, we were now in a huge snag forest, and tall dead pines stood all around like ghostly sentinels. As darkness fell, their dead bark took on an eerie aspect from the setting sun muted behind the thick clouds.

We looked and looked, but we couldn't find anywhere to camp where there weren't snags. It was as close to dark as we could get and still see to set up our tents, and we had to stop.

I was exhausted, but Rowdy acted like he could hike all night. In fact, he suggested we do just that, since he didn't want to camp in the snags. In a former lifetime, the one before I met the shaggy hiker by Trapper's Lake, I might have agreed to do that, but not now—I was just too tired and on edge, and I didn't want to chance getting lost. I told Rowdy we'd just have to take our chances with dying from deadfall. He said it was an interesting play on words, then reluctantly took off his pack.

We set up the tents in a thinner part of the forest, but we were still surrounded by dead pine—some stood thirty or forty feet tall. We could see where a number had already fallen.

I pretty much collapsed into my sleeping bag, so tired I didn't even want dinner. I don't remember much, except waking once to the eerie sound of trees creaking and seeing long shadows across my tent. I awoke at dawn to a distant sound that sounded like a tree crashing to the ground, then went back to sleep. It wasn't until Rowdy woke me with a cup of coffee that I really came around.

I drank it while still in my bag, then mustered the energy to get up. It was cold, and I could see my breath. Rowdy already had his tent down and pack ready, though it was still early. He seemed unusually quiet and eager to get going. He made me more hot coffee and some hot oatmeal while I broke camp. It was now totally gray and dreary, speaking to the leading edge of a huge storm.

"What's up, Bud?" I asked. Rowdy usually lounged around camp until I made the push to go.

"Nothing, just feeling like we need to get going."

"Anything in particular?"

"The weather, among other things," he answered. He pointed to a dusting of fresh snow on the cliffs above us.

I asked, "What other things?"

Rowdy was quiet for awhile, then asked, "Didn't you hear the noises last night?"

"I heard the snags creaking, that's all."

"Wood knocking," he replied quietly.

"Holy crap," I said. "Are you sure?"

"Yup. For a long time. They got closer and closer. There were at least three of them, all in different directions. I'm thinking we need to turn around and go back now."

"What? We're way over halfway now," I replied.

"Yeah, but we know the way back. The way forward is unknown. We can make better time if we turn around."

Rowdy was scared, and so was I, but we needed to push forward, not turn around, especially with this storm. We were only a day or two, at the most, from our destination.

I answered, "You're wanting the security of the known, but we're not that far out now. We have to go forward. If we go back, we'll run out of supplies. And we'd have to keep really close bearings, as things always look different when you're hiking the opposite direction. We can't make enough faster time to justify it."

We both sat there awhile, uncertain of what to do. It now started to drizzle, a cold rain that felt like ice.

Rowdy added, "If we go forward, we still have to cross the Devil's Causeway, though we'll come out sooner. But the Causeway will be a real bear if it's snow or ice covered. It's scary enough when it's dry."

The Devil's Causeway was part of the Chinese Wall, a huge volcanic dike that we would have to hike across at an altitude of almost 12,000 feet. The Chinese Wall was about

200 feet wide, but the Devil's Causeway portion was very exposed and narrow—a mere three feet across for about 20 feet, and 400 sheer feet down on either side.

We had both hiked it from the other side when we were in high school. It was very rocky and difficult under the best of conditions, and we'd seen seasoned hikers cower and turn around because of the exposure. The views were like being in an airplane. Of course, there would be no views in this storm.

I suspected that we would be in a full-out blizzard by the time we got to the Chinese Wall, and I knew Rowdy suspected the same, but neither of us said a word. We both stood, put on our packs, and started down the trail, going forward.

It was now sleeting and cold, and the trail was slippery. We had good coats, but we both felt chilled to the bone from the damp. After a couple of hours, we stopped to make hot chocolate.

As we sat there boiling water on our little backpacking stove, I heard it—wood knocking, just like Rowdy had said, and not so far away. I felt even more chilled. The hiker's words "You wouldn't be the first ones to just disappear out there," kept running through my mind.

Rowdy had heard it also. We quickly drank the hot chocolate and headed out, our walking gait turning into a half-jog, even though it was wet and slick. We found some large sticks and used them to help keep our balance.

Soon it was dusk. We'd made good time and had to be close to the Chinese Wall. The wet drizzle was now turning into snow. And I had another first in my life—for the first time, I thought I could die out there in the wilderness. It occurred to me how truly easy it would be, which I think fueled some sort of survival instinct, as I told Rowdy we were going to try our hands at night hiking and hope we didn't get lost. He agreed it was a swell idea.

We'd hike by headlamp until we got to the Chinese Wall, then regroup. Pure insanity, but we were both chilled to the bone at the thought of spending a night in camp surrounded by Wood Knockers.

We picked up the pace, but as it became dark, we stopped long enough to eat a hot dinner. We both knew it was the smart thing to do, as our bodies needed fuel and warmth to continue on. I could see us both wandering, lost, hypothermic, in a blizzard, and it seemed to be a prophetic vision at this point.

As we set there, eating freeze-dried stew and drinking hot tea, the wind picked up and the forest began to creak. We were in more snags, and the storm was now moving in full brunt.

Just then, what sounded like a huge tree came crashing to the ground not more than twenty feet from us, so close we both were barraged by small branches that snapped off from the impact. Time to go.

We slogged on in the dark, following somewhat of a trail through the tall grasses and trees, and finally, at what I guessed to be about two a.m., we reached some rocky rubble, what I suspected to be the beginnings of a talus slope. If so, this was the trail up the Chinese Wall and would soon become a steep and treacherous rocky climb. We had to stop. We couldn't navigate this in the dark, and we needed to rest. We were both exhausted.

We were at the edge of another snag forest, so we began collecting wood. We would try to rest and get warm around a big fire. It was still sleeting and thus difficult to find dry wood, but we knew if we got the fire going hot enough, even damp wood would burn.

We soon had a huge pile of wood from the nearby forest, enough to build a big bonfire. We didn't even bother to put up our tents, but instead draped them over us to keep us dry, laying our sleeping bags next to the fire, which raged and helped warm us up.

We decided to take turns keeping the fire going, as the last thing we wanted was for it to go out. I knew Rowdy was exhausted, so I offered to stand first watch. I also figured the odds were better of the fire being fed if I stayed up and let him sleep, as I didn't trust him to stay awake.

To make a long story short, I fell asleep myself, and the fire went out. I awoke sometime later with a start, as something had made my instincts kick in. I lay there very still and could soon hear a large animal pacing back and forth in the darkness, not far away, crashing through the brush and snapping sticks. It seemed unhappy that we were here.

Just then, something whizzed by my head, something big, which then crashed into the grasses behind us. I jumped up and quickly got the fire going again.

The Wood Knockers had followed us—I knew it was them. What else could throw something like that?

Whoosh! Another snag came flying through the air, a big one. It almost landed in the fire. I started yelling and cussing, both from fright and anger. We'd finally almost made it out, and now these creatures were going to kill us.

Death by deadfall, except it didn't fall. No one would believe it. Death by snag missile—what a way to go.

Now Rowdy was up, next to the fire, scared to death, chilled and teeth chattering.

Wham! Another tree came in, but not quite as close. These creatures must be huge and strong to throw something like a snag. The thought of all this made me want to start crying. All the stress and physical exhaustion of the past few days had taken their toll.

I started yelling again, at the top of my lungs. I had no idea what time of night it was, but dawn couldn't be too far off.

All of a sudden, what I heard made my teeth start chattering along with Rowdy's. It was a blood-curdling scream like nothing on this planet. It sounded angry and like it wanted to kill us. And it went on and on, at a volume that defied all reason, echoing through the cliffs and on and on into the deep thickness of the forest behind us.

I knew we were dead, then and there. In fact, I took Rowdy and put my arm around his shoulder. I could feel his chest heaving, and I knew he was silently sobbing.

I softly told him, "Whatever happens, Bro, we're going to get through this. You watch. We're sons of guns, and we're survivors."

What I really wanted to say was goodbye, see you on the other side—but I didn't want to make him worse.

The screaming had dissolved, just like a huge ocean wave slams the shore and gradually dissipates. But the weird feeling it left behind really messed with my mind. I just couldn't believe this was happening.

"We have to go now," I told Rowdy. "Let's leave the fire burning as a decoy and see if we can slip away. It's got to be near dawn. If we can get across the Chinese Wall, maybe they'll leave us alone."

"Why would that matter?" Rowdy asked.

"Territory," I answered, although I didn't believe it myself. "Besides, better to die fighting than huddling by a fire."

We banked the fire as high as we could, grabbed our packs, and slipped off. Snow sizzled into the fire behind us—it was really starting to come down now. I seriously doubted we could get out, even without Wood Knockers to distract us.

We stopped, and I shone my light ahead. The falling snow made it difficult to tell, but I had been right, we were at the base of the Chinese Wall, the beginnings of a talus slope that I knew was steep and unstable. It would be twice as tricky with snow on it. We started climbing, wondering if the Wood Knockers were behind. I knew they were.

We carefully made our way upward as dawn broke. I was glad to see the light, as I knew that even if we could get up the talus slope, traversing the actual Chinese Wall in the dark would be dangerous, as one had to stay to the middle—it was a sheer drop off on either side, although wide. But when it narrowed to a mere three feet at the Devil's Causeway, it would be pure suicide in the dark and ice.

It was now snowing hard, and the winds whipped it into swirling clouds, howling, and I sometimes thought I could hear a Wood Knocker scream through it. Visibility was poor in the dawning light, but we just climbed up and up until we reached the top and it began to level out. We were now on the actual Chinese Wall. We stopped to catch our breath and knock the snow off our packs, but we didn't stop for long.

"Rowdy," I whispered, "There's something coming up behind us. Gotta go fast now." I grabbed his arm and pulled him along, half running and half slipping. I could hear footsteps behind us, a heavy pounding sound like something big, when the wind quit whistling and whipping our coats long enough to hear anything. I was terrified.

We both ran as fast as we could, sliding along, and fortunately we could now see well enough to stay in the middle of the Wall. I didn't dare turn around to see what seemed to be rapidly catching up to us.

Now we were at the narrow nightmare called the Devil's Causeway. Rowdy stopped, frozen in fear. The 20 foot catwalk was covered with several inches of snow— rubbly rocks made the going hazardous enough, without adding snow—and the visibility was poor, but we could still see the sheer drop off on both sides.

The wind seemed to be worse, and I figured it was because of the narrowness here, it was coming straight up from either side and meeting in the middle. I now began to think the wind was more of a danger to us than the snow, as it would mess with our balance and whip us right off.

"Go, Rowdy, go!" I screamed. I had now turned around just enough to see something huge and black behind us, although I couldn't make out what it was because of the blinding snow.

But Rowdy stood frozen. We could now hear the Wood Knocker making grunting noises, and it was quickly gaining on us. We had to act fast.

"Ditch your pack!" I screamed into the wind, throwing my heavy pack into the abyss below. Rowdy quickly did the same, as he knew it would make the crossing easier. We might regret not having our survival gear, but not as much as we would regret falling.

I hooked my arm through Rowdy's, and we quickly yet deliberately walked across, not daring to look down. At one point, I could feel myself starting to slip, but he grabbed me, and I miraculously recovered. It was the longest 20 feet of my life. The wind nearly blew us off, but I think we had more stability because we were hanging onto each other for dear life.

Finally, we were across!

I turned, scared to death at what I knew I would see, then stunned by what I actually did see.

Something big was coming across the Causeway, not more than 30 feet from us. Rowdy saw it and began yelling something unintelligible. We should've both started running, but we were frozen in fear, literally. It was hard to make out its features through the thick snowfall, but we both knew it was a Wood Knocker, a Bigfoot.

But the creature hadn't gone more than a few feet across when an especially strong gust of wind hit it, and it started to lose its footing. We watched in horror as it balanced for a moment and then, seemingly in slow motion, began falling off the side, its last movement a horrible grasping at the rocks with its long arms flailing.

It let out a long terrifying scream as it fell, and to think of it takes my breath away even to this day.

And what happened next I also couldn't believe.

We heard gunshots. Someone was on the Chinese Wall not far ahead of us, shooting what sounded like a rifle. The shots popped, and the sound echoed back and forth. Someone was nearby!

Rowdy and I both started yelling at the top of our lungs. We yelled and yelled until we thought we would go hoarse. We yelled as we hightailed it down the far side of the Chinese Wall. We wanted whoever it was to find us.

We soon saw two figures through the wind-whipped snow. It was now a full-on blizzard. How they found us I'll never know, but it was my Uncle Joe and Rowdy's stepdad. They'd come looking for us. They had a base camp set up not too far away, complete with horses and food.

They'd hoped to meet us on our way out, and came as soon as my uncle had realized what was really coming in weather wise. He'd fortunately helped us plot our route, so had an idea of where we would be. He had watched the forecast like a hawk, and when he realized how huge a storm was coming in, he knew we would need help.

We were never happier to see other human beings. We returned to the camp, got warmed up, ate a hot meal, then headed out on horses, making good time. Riding never felt so good, even though I was sore for days afterwards.

We later found out the high Flattops got six feet of snow from that storm. Our mountain man days were over. Forever.

It was a few years later that Rowdy and I decided to get my uncle to ride in with us to check it all out. He brought horses, and we came in from the Yampa side, along the base of the Chinese Wall, right to where we could look up and see the Devil's Causeway. Even though it was a warm

summer day, I could still feel the chill of that early morning, high up there in the blizzard, holding onto Rowdy and
watching the Wood Knocker scream as it fell.

I found only one thing from our packs, and that was a
tin cup I had carried that said "Lone Joe's Outfitting." There
was otherwise no trace of anything. I knew we'd thrown
our packs off that side, so it was kind of weird. We looked
around a bit for bones, but never found any.

It seems we all got the creeps at the same time, cause
everyone decided to turn around and go back, instead of
having the picnic lunch we'd brought along. We rode back,
loaded up the horses, and had a nice dinner at the Antler's
Bar in Yampa, then went on back to Meeker.

[2] Tired of Tourists

· ·

I've been up into Canada several times, but always with a pretty good sized group of people, and I've never had the chance to really do any Squatchin'. But based on the Canadian stories I've heard, the Bigfoot up there, which they often call Sasquatch, aren't nearly as amiable as the ones this side of the border.

This story came from a fellow who called himself Crow, and why he called himself that I never did find out, but he was a heckuvva fisherman. I enjoyed his story, though it did leave me feeling a bit uncomfortable about traveling alone in the Canadian Rockies. —Rusty

My story took place in the summer of 2010, in early August. I was between jobs (as in unemployed), so I decided to take some of my savings and do something I've always wanted to do—go to Canada. I've always wanted to see the Canadian Rockies.

So, I got my passport and, since I have three dogs, I got their shots all current along with the veterinarian exam papers that Canada requires. After all that, I was never asked to see the dogs' papers, but I sure didn't want to risk not being legal.

I live in Wyoming, so I decided to just head north and see the country at a leisurely pace. I went through the Tetons and Yellowstone and finally arrived in Glacier National Park about three weeks later. I was an old hand at camping, having done it since I was a kid.

I was camped kind of illegally in Glacier, way out on a back dirt road off the highway that loops from St. Mary's around to Hungry Horse, the back road that most tourists don't take, as they want to go over the Going to the Sun Road.

It was a sweet camp, and I'd set up my big tent and all, and I knew nobody ever went in there because the grasses were growing so high you could barely find the road, which ended at my campsite. And man, what views! I could look down and see St. Mary's Lake and huge distant waterfalls from my tent door. It was paradise.

Because of finding this great spot, I decided I'd go up into Waterton National Park in Canada, and make it a one day trip instead of packing up and then trying to find a camp spot up there. A friend who had been up there told me that the park would be very crowded that time of year.

I wanted to spend most of my time in Canada in Banff and Jasper National Parks, and I wanted to backtrack through Montana and cross the border north of Kalispell, so I wanted to come back down that way anyway, no need to change camps.

I got up really early, made some coffee, filled my thermos, fed the dogs, grabbed some lunch stuff, then we all jumped into my pickup and headed for Canada. It was a beautiful drive, and we crossed the border with no problems and were soon coming down the grade into Waterton.

I couldn't believe the size of these mountains, even though I'd just been in Glacier, they seemed bigger and even more magnificent. I had to stop several times to just sit and stare.

Well, I made it into Waterton, and boy, was I disappointed. The park advertises itself as a quiet untrammeled place, and I suppose it is in general, but the little town of Waterton is a tourist trap bar none. It was hard to even find a place to turn around, and the streets were packed with people walking around, with nowhere to even park.

I drove around a bit, checked out the little waterfall there, then left, heading for Cameron Lake, which is at the end of a windy road that climbs high in the mountains above Waterton.

The lake was beautiful with a white glacier hanging above its far shores, but once again, it was crowded with people. You could rent canoes there, and the lake was just hopping with boats. I found a little side trail that I had no idea where it went, but it said dogs were allowed, so I put everyone on leashes and headed out. They needed a hike.

I hadn't got more than 50 feet when I was greeted by a group of about 20 people coming up the trail, yelling and laughing and all that. I don't usually mind people, but—well, OK, I do mind people when I want solitude, and I especially wanted to let the dogs stretch their legs a bit. This wasn't the place.

We got back in the truck and headed back down the windy road. I was too busy watching the road and dodging RVs to even see much of the scenery, and there were almost no places to turn off and get out, so that was kind of a blur.

I decided to go see a place called Red Rock Canyon. It was the opposite direction from how I'd come into the park, so I turned left at the bottom of the hill and let everyone else go on back to Waterton. Good riddance.

Red Rock Canyon sounded attractive to me because the name reminded me a bit of the Red Rock Desert in Wyoming. I guess I was getting a bit homesick by that time. The Canadian Rockies are all sedimentary rocks, not granite or volcanic, which makes them truly spectacular because they have lots of layers and colors. Red Rock Canyon sounded like a place I should see.

One thing I'd discovered about Waterton was that you could hike with your dogs, unlike the national parks in the U.S., which I found to be a very cool thing about Canada.

Well, there wasn't much traffic on the Red Rock road, which was nice, and it wasn't all narrow and windy, once you got up above the highway a bit. It kind of went through a big wide valley with a nice creek running through with lots of willows. A good place for moose, I remember thinking, though I never did see any.

I hope I'm not going into too much detail here and boring you, but I really want to paint a picture of how it was.

Anyway, I hadn't gone more than a few miles when I saw a sign saying that the road to the canyon was closed at a certain point for construction. Great, no Red Rock Canyon for me. I was getting kind of fed up with Waterton National Peace Park, as Canada called it, pretty as it was.

By now, I really needed to get the dogs out. I spied a campground to the left across the creek, so I turned in there, but the sign said full, so I just turned around and went on down the road. Too many people everywhere. You have to remember that I'm from Wyoming, and there's almost no one around where I live, so I'm not used to many people.

Before long, I came to a turnout that had a historical marker, so I stopped there. I read the marker, and I can only recall that it was something about the natives there and some explorer, but I don't recall anything about who or when.

I let the dogs out for a minute, and they went into the bushes and did their thing, then I decided this would be a great spot to get them out for some exercise.

I was kind of wishing I'd just stayed at my camp in Glacier, as we would've had a nice day just goofing around there, but on the other hand, at least I'd seen Waterton now, or a bit of it, anyway. But we were used to getting out, and we needed some exercise.

We headed up a big hill that appeared to be part of the foothills of a big mountain that rose above them, I mean a really big mountain. It was beautiful, all layered in various shades of red.

The dogs were really happy to be out, and we all kind of bounded up this big hill for a bit. I had to stop and catch my breath, and the views were stunning. I was really enjoying this and now liking Waterton, and so were the dogs.

But all of a sudden, the dogs stopped cold. They just stood there, looking ahead, and as I came up behind them,

I could see that the one closest to me, Otis, was shaking. I've never seen my dogs shake. I then noticed they were all shaking. Before I could even say a word, two of them had turned and were hightailing it back to the truck as fast as they could go. We hadn't come very far, so they were back down there really fast, and I could see them crawling under the truck.

Now Otis was running back, too. He was very protective of me, and I'd never seen him do anything like that. I decided it must be a big grizzly bear, and maybe they could smell it, where I couldn't, and I'd better pay attention, so I was soon also heading back at a good clip.

I unlocked the truck and everyone jumped in, which was unusual, as I typically have to get after them, they always want to fiddle around, smell everything. I jumped in and locked the doors.

Now I started scanning the hill, wondering why we were all so scared. I finally rolled down my window, but I didn't hear or see anything. By now another car had pulled up to read the sign, and they smiled at me and got out and acted like everything was fine.

I was puzzled. What had the dogs sensed or smelled?

I've been a bit of a photographer since I was a kid, even though I never could afford nice equipment. But most of my stuff was landscape photos, as there wasn't much where I lived except deer and antelope in the sense of wildlife.

But ever since going through Yellowstone, I'd come to understand why people are so attracted to wildlife photography. I'd taken some photos there of wolves and buffalo and even a huge great-horned owl. So, I was kind of hoping this grizzly would come out to where I could get some photos—from the safety of my truck, anyway, and where I could get away fast.

I set there a bit, even though the dogs were again shivering. I have a club cab, and Sunny and Maggie were in the back, hiding on the floor. My dogs are all labs, and they're happy-go-lucky, and I don't think they think enough about things to get scared much. Even fireworks don't usually bother them. So I knew this had to be something really scary.

I rolled the windows back up. The other car left. I started the pickup and turned it so I could make a quick getaway, if needed, then turned it off and just sat there. Whatever it was, it was still around, according to the dogs. I got my camera ready to go.

By now, it was getting on towards late afternoon. It had been a long day, and I wanted to take a picture of this grizz, then I would head back to Glacier.

Just then, something huge jumped onto the back of my truck. I have a camper shell, so whatever it was, it had to have jumped onto the bumper. The whole front end of the truck came up, including the front wheels. We just hung there in the air for a minute.

I was shocked and dropped my camera. I couldn't see what was holding the truck up, but it was something big. I hadn't seen anything coming, which was really strange, as I kept looking around and in the rear-view mirrors.

Just then, I heard a breaking sound. My truck was falling apart! The front came down with a wham and I nearly smashed my nose on the steering wheel.

I had the presence of mind to start the truck and slam it into gear and peel out while I could. Dirt and rocks went flying into the air, and I know they must've hit this thing in the face, as it had to be standing directly behind me.

As I peeled out onto the blacktop, I felt something slam against the side of the truck, and I saw a big tree branch rolling down the road behind me. By then, I had the accelerator floored and was quickly getting up speed. But not fast enough, because I noticed something in my passenger-side rear mirror, and this really shook me up.

Something big and human-like was chasing me, wearing a fur coat, and it had nearly caught up. It looked like it was trying to grab onto the door handle. I reached down and hit the auto-lock, making sure all the doors were locked. By now, Otis was whining his head off in the seat beside me. Maggie and Sunny were still on the floor, so I couldn't see them at all.

By now, my truck had ramped up and we were finally able to leave this thing behind. I never did get a really good look at it, but I can tell you this—it was no grizzly. What I did see was that it was huge and covered in light brown, long, flowing hair. It was a Canadian Sasquatch, and you can believe me or not—it doesn't matter either way, because I know what I saw.

I drove like a madman towards Red Rock Canyon, the direction I'd had the truck pointed. I'd forgotten the road would be closed, so I was surprised when I got a mile or two down the road and saw a flagger ahead, wearing orange. It was a woman, and she stopped me and told me I had to turn around and go back.

I was in shock, and I told her I couldn't turn around and go back. I hardly knew what I was saying. She said I had to turn around, as they were working on the road. I just sat there. Finally, another car came up behind me, so I decided I would turn around, then follow it back. There was no way I was going through that stretch of road alone.

I turned around and pulled over to let the other car go around me. It then dawned on me that I should get out and see how much damage my truck had taken. What I saw really messed with my mind—my entire bumper was gone! And there was a big dent where the tree branch had hit, just above the wheel well.

It also dawned on me that I needed to get that bumper back, as it had my license plate on it. I would get pulled over with no plate, and what was I to say, that a Sasquatch had torn it off? I had to stop back there and get it. But I couldn't, there was no way.

About then, a pickup came along with Montana plates, and I flagged it down. I explained that I'd lost my bumper back down the road, and I needed someone to help me load it into my truck—would they mind following along and helping? The driver was a real nice guy, he looked like a rancher or something, and he said he would.

I hoped I wasn't getting them involved in something bad, but when I got to the pullover I slowed down, did a quick look around, then pulled over. Sure enough, my bumper lay there, all twisted up, but the plate was still on it. I hoped the Squatch had moved on.

The guy from Montana got out and asked me what had happened, but I couldn't tell him the truth, so I said

I'd backed into a rock and hadn't realized it until later. He looked skeptical, but helped me load it into the back of my truck.

I couldn't wait to get out of there, especially after I smelled a strong skunky odor. I thanked him, then he asked me if I was OK. I decided to tell him the truth, so I quickly told him what had happened. He commented on the strong odor, and then jumped into his truck and drove away. I think he believed me. I was right behind him.

The drive back was a blur. I don't really remember anything, not even the border crossing. By the time I got back to Montana and the little resort town of St. Mary, I had had it. No way did I have the courage to go back to my camp, so I rented a room, no matter that it was really expensive and I had to sneak the dogs in. I didn't care.

The next day, I drove back to my camp. What I saw scared the heck out of me. All around the tent were huge bear tracks. I know it was a grizzly. It hadn't bothered anything, but had just walked around a bunch.

I was then glad I'd stayed at the motel, because if I'd come back, who knows what would've happened. Maybe that was why nobody had camped there for so long, it was prime grizz territory.

I packed everything up and headed home. I'd go see Banff and Jasper another day, which I did, but from the comfort of motel rooms at night. I've never camped since, except in the desert.

But I've often wondered if that Squatch hadn't felt like I did that day—sick of tourists everywhere.

[3] The Blue Lakes Bigfoot

Since I'm based in Colorado, I get my share of people from that great state wanting to learn to fly fish. Consequently, I have a lot of stories in my collection from the San Juan Mountains. Here's another good one, told over a cold beer in a popular Ridgway, Colorado restaurant.

Interestingly enough, not long after I heard this story, a friend who had recently found Bigfoot tracks in the Weiminuche Wilderness of the southern San Juans called and told me of being harassed by a Bigfoot all night while camped at the same Blue Lakes as in this story. Apparently it just walked around and around his tent, making huffing noises. He had just asked his girlfriend to marry him that day, so it was a pretty memorable occasion for them both, lying there in the tent terrified all night.
—Rusty

If you hang around the Sneffels Range of Colorado's San Juan Mountains very long, you'll hear people mention the Blue Lakes Bigfoot—or maybe you'll meet him yourself.

This thing has scared hikers, climbers, and backpackers in that area for many years. He's a legend by now, although it's all word of mouth.

The local tourism people will tell you it's a joke, as they don't want people being scared away, but I know it exists. I know because I saw him. My name's Dennis, and my story happened about five years ago.

My brother Kevin and I had been wanting to climb Mt. Sneffels for a number of years, but we never could get everything together to go do it. Seems like there was always some reason we couldn't. We were both in high school at the time, and this 14,150-foot peak was right in our back yard, almost, as we lived in Ouray. It was kind of embarrassing to tell people we were climbers from Ouray and had never summited Sneffels.

Finally, one beautiful late summer day, we headed up to the base of Blue Lakes Pass to climb the peak. There are two ways one can climb, and we chose the longer one, simply because the other route, from Yankee Boy Basin, required a high-clearance vehicle, which we didn't have. We were driving an old Subaru, and just getting it into the Blue Lakes trailhead about killed the darn thing. Lots of rocks and places on that road that aren't so great.

We arrived at the trailhead around nine a.m. We wanted to get up to the upper lake to camp, then summit the next day, camp below it again, then come back down to the car. It was a reasonable plan, as the Blue Lakes route is longer and harder than the Yankee Boy route, and camping at the upper lake would make the summit much closer. Mt. Sneffles looms over the lakes, reminding you of what a fool you are to try to climb it.

Blue Lakes are three glaciated lakes that sit like gems under Mt. Sneffels, which is said to be the most photographed peak in the Colorado Rockies. It's very photogenic and spectacular, and the lakes are that glacier blue that comes from particulates suspended in the water.

The lakes are high one above the other, and you can't see all three until you're up above them looking down. And getting up high above them like that requires climbing Blue Lakes Pass, which is a narrow and exposed trail winding up the side of a huge saddle that connects Mt. Sneffels to Gilpin Peak and that separates the drainages between Yankee Boy and Blue Lakes.

That pass is scary if you're carrying a backpack, as the trail is narrow and one misstep and you're going to tumble for a good six-hundred feet. We planned to turn at the top of it and climb Sneffels, then retrace our route. We would camp at the upper lake, leaving our heavy packs there.

So, we parked at the trailhead, got out our gear, ate some of the required gorp all backpackers carry, fed the chipmunks a bit, then headed out. We had plenty of time to lolly gag and look around, as the hike to the upper lake was a little over four miles, and though a steep uphill at about 2,400 feet gain, we could easily do that and set up camp in a day. We would start at 9,350 feet and end up at 11,720 at the upper lake.

We crossed the log bridge over East Dallas Creek, which was roaring from late snowmelt, then headed up the trail. It took awhile to get our second wind, even though we were in good shape and were used to high altitudes, living and hiking around Ouray.

We took our time and were soon at the middle lake, the smaller of the three, where we stopped and drank some power drinks and then skipped rocks across the powder-blue waters. The lake sits in a huge cirque, and there was snow coming right down into the lake on the other side, up against the mountain's scree flanks.

It was so beautiful we talked about camping there, but we knew we'd pay the price the next day if we didn't carry on up to the higher lake. After a half-hour or so, just long enough to lose our momentum, we put on our big backpacks and resumed our trek.

Now the trail skirted around the side of the lake and was consistently steep, whereas before it had been steep in spurts. We were soon winded again and had to go slow. We climbed high above the second lake and had tremendous views of it and the flanks of Sneffels.

We were now above timberline, and the trail finally leveled out into a rich carpet of alpine tundra, dotted with wildflowers of every description. We were high in the upper basin, a meadow surrounded by 13,000-foot ridges that were punctuated by Mt. Sneffels, Dallas Peak, and Gilpin Peak. It was a tremendous place to be, in the true sense of the word. We were the only ones there, and we just sat down for awhile, basking in the solitude and beauty.

We arrived at the upper lake, then decided to hike a bit away from it, up onto a higher plateau at the base of Blue Lakes Pass, which we could now see crisscrossing the ridge high above us. For some reason, it looked foreboding. The peaks above us also looked foreboding, with their jagged rugged pinnacles and volcanic spires. The San Juans were created by volcanic forces, and here, one could really see the black rocks and serrated ridges.

We dropped our packs at what looked like a good place to camp, a small wide hollow filled with columbine and shooting stars and daisies. I hated to even put my pack down, for fear of smashing a flower, but I finally found a place where it was all tundra, right by the trail. Kevin set his tent up by the trail also, but a little bit away from mine so my snoring wouldn't bother him.

It was now early afternoon, and we were hungry, so we took out bread and peanut butter and jelly and made sandwiches. While sitting there eating, we noted that wispy gray clouds were beginning to curl around the big peaks above us. It would be wise to set up camp now, we decided. The weather forecast had been generally good, but we were now in monsoon season, when afternoon thunderstorms would come rolling through.

Our little backpacking tents were soon up, and fatigue hit us hard. We crawled inside, intending to take a little nap. Altitude does that to one, makes you really sleepy from the lack of oxygen.

I don't know how long I slept, but I awoke to a crack followed by booming thunder, and I jumped up, sticking my head out my tent flap just in time to see a marmot dragging our loaf of bread away at breakneck speed. I knew I should run out and get it, as we hadn't brought a second loaf, but I was too scared, as just then another bolt hit a small spire right in my line of sight. It was a huge wide bolt, and the thunder was deafening.

There we sat, in our tents, right in what looked to be a major lightning storm. The San Juans have a very high iron content and are like a magnet for lightning. The most spectacular lightning I've ever seen has been in the San Juans, and I've done a lot of traveling, including spending a summer in Tampa, Florida, the supposed lightning capitol of the world. I think the San Juan bolts are much bigger, at least they look that way. And it's truly terrifying to be that exposed in a storm with nowhere to hide. The thunder just echoes forever off those high peaks.

I yelled at Kevin, but he seemed to still be sleeping. I decided if he was tired enough to sleep through that kind of racket, I'd let him sleep.

Craaack, another huge bolt hit, but now nearby in the meadow. I counted to 2 before the thunder started. That was close. Five seconds was a mile.

As much camping as I've done, I've never figured out if you're safer in or out of a tent. I just sat in my tent, hoping the poles wouldn't act as lightning rods, looking out through the flap. It was getting darker by the minute as huge black clouds moved in.

I could see Blue Lakes Pass from inside my tent, and suddenly movement way up on the upper pass caught my eye. Oh man, someone was up there, right in the thick of things! Poor guy, he was sure to get hit!

I watched as he came down the first switchback. Boom, lightning strike, not far from him. I expected him to crouch down, which is what's recommended when caught in lightning, but he just kept coming down the pass. It looked like he was carrying a huge pack.

Just then, Kevin came tumbling into my tent. He was now wide awake and terrified. He really thought we were going to die up there, and to be honest, so did I.

I pointed out the figure on the pass to him. Kaboom! More lightning. It was now popping around us everywhere. I've never seen anything like that storm before or since. And the hiker just kept coming down the pass. We were sure we were about to witness death by lightning, his and maybe also ours.

Kevin remarked at the hiker's stupidity to keep going and not crouch down, but I said I thought that his odds were better once he got off that pass, so maybe he was doing the right thing. Of course, it's just a matter of odds anyway when you're in a storm like that.

Now this guy was about two-thirds down the pass, where we could get a better look at him. For some reason, it only then struck us that he was coming down at a tremendous speed without actually running. We found this weird. How could he get down the pass so fast without running?

Now Kevin was getting nervous. He pointed out that the guy wasn't carrying a pack, but was just really huge. What we'd thought was a pack was his shoulders and head. We watched him carefully, and as he came closer, sure enough, we could see clearly that he was a really big guy.

More lightning, not far from him, but the guy didn't even pause. He just kept coming down the switchbacks. And now we were beginning to make him out better. His arms seemed extraordinarily long, and they hung way down, almost to his knees. And his stride was huge! And now we could see he was all in black. He had very muscular legs that looked like a football player's.

We both were starting to get the creeps. This was no fellow backpacker, this was something out of our range of recognizable reality. And we were camped almost on the trail. It would soon be coming right by our tents. And there were no trees to run and hide in, nothing.

Now I looked towards some motion towards the lake, and what I saw was almost as scary. A huge sheet of white was coming at us at a rapid clip! I yelled to Kevin, and we both bailed out of the tent and grabbed our packs, dragging them into our tents. Kevin zipped his tent up and rejoined me in mine. He didn't even have time to get his jacket out before it hit—torrential rain! I zipped up my tent flap to keep us dry, no idea where the big black creature was by now, and pulled my wool sweater out, giving it to Kevin while I put on my jacket. I wondered where the big black creature was going.

It blew and poured and popped and I thought we were going to die for sure, but my little tent held up. The rain eventually stopped, and by now it was almost black outside, it was so dark. I finally stuck my head out of the tent flap to see what was going on. I couldn't believe my eyes—it was snowing!

That was the final straw. We decided to bail and try to get out. We had no idea where the black thing was, but we had to get out. We quickly rolled up our little tents and stuffed them into our packs and headed down the trail. It was only about four in the afternoon, but the dark clouds made it seem like late evening.

The trail out was slick and treacherous, but at least it wasn't exposed, so we were able to make good time, slipping along in the snowy mud. The huge nearby cliffs had waterfalls pouring off them, a sight I've never seen before or since. It was awesome.

We got down to the middle lake when we came upon the tracks. The snow had turned into a light rain, and there, in the mud, were huge five-toed tracks, heading right down the trail ahead of us. Kevin put his boot into one, and it easily engulfed it.

I can tell you that this really terrified us. That thing had walked right past us, and now we were behind it. We just stood there, not knowing what to do. It was still a good hike back to the car. What if we ran into it?

Kevin was now shivering, but I wasn't sure if it was from the cold or from fear—maybe both. I told him that whatever it was, if it wanted to harm us, it would have done so when it came by us in our tents. It could have easily killed us both right then and there. This seemed to help some, and we started down the trail, though a bit slower and more warily.

It didn't seem to take us long to get back to the car and stow our packs away. The sun was out now, and we were wondering if we'd made the right decision, coming out and abandoning ship. We sat there awhile, talking about everything, when what we heard next made us certain our decision was the right one.

Not far away, we heard a loud who-hoot, who-hoot, followed by the same, but from behind us a ways. These were not owls, but the voices of something larger than us, something completely at home in these extreme environments where we occasionally tread, calling it adventure, then going home to our safe houses and towns, where everything is controlled.

Out there, we're no longer the omnipotent ones, even with our equipment and guns and high-tech survival gear. We're nothing compared to those great beasts who live at ease in harsh weather like what we'd just been through.

It was time for us to go home and leave this place to those who belonged here.

We heard an eerie howl as we got into the car and drove away.

[4] The Bigfoot Buffet

We were sitting around a campfire in that beautiful country along the Gallatin River near Bozeman, Montana when I heard this story. The teller, a guy named Cody, had grown up in that area, and had even helped a bit with the movie "A River Runs Through It," which was filmed not far from where we were. When someone said this looked like Bigfoot country, this is the story he told. And since it took place not too far from where we were, I can tell you we all kind of kept our eyes open after that. —Rusty

I used to be an avid bowhunter, going out into places people seldom if ever ventured. Nobody ever tells a bow-hunter to never hunt alone, to take someone along like they do when you're a hiker—it's a solitary sport, and that's why I enjoyed it. I think it was also the man versus nature thing, seeing if you could survive your own wayfinding and weather reading. This was back before everyone carried a GPS.

Of course, all this was when I was younger, and now my only sport is flyfishing, and I never go alone. Let me tell you why I switched sports and philosophies.

I was in my early thirties and in extraordinary shape. I worked construction, and that kept me hopping. I was also a distance runner, so I had a good set of legs and lungs. I got into distance running when I was in high school, and I just kept at it. It helped me clear my mind, especially when I had problems. I would go out and just run and run.

Good thing, as I believe these things are what kept me alive that day in late September, a good twenty years back. I was in the kind of shape one needs to be to make an escape, which fortunately I did—obviously, or I wouldn't be telling this story.

I was hunting in the thick timber in the Bridger Mountains of Montana, above Bozeman. Even though the area's close to a pretty good-sized town, as you get further away, it becomes the kind of wild country where seeing another human kind of makes you startle. I was up above what's called Fairy Lake, if you know where that is. I read not too long ago of another sighting there at the lake, and people should be aware of what's up there and just stay away, if they know what's best.

I was all dressed in green cammies and was just quietly walking through the forest up there, looking for signs of deer, as it was the start of deer bowhunting season. I had just enough blaze orange on me to tell someone not to shoot, just a patch of orange flagging tied onto my cap. I would stop every so often and just hang out, hoping a deer would come by.

Well, it was a bit before dawn, and I had hiked up the side of this one big drainage for about an hour, using a headlamp to see my way until it got light. I wanted to be ready, up in the high timber, when the sun came up. It's hard to hike like that in the dark, and you'd better have a good sense of direction, or you'll end up where you don't want to be. But the early predawn light told me which way was east and I was doing OK, coming up right where I wanted to, once I could see enough to tell.

I stopped and watched as the early light started opening things up a bit. I had slipped behind a tree, as was my habit when hunting, and all of a sudden I could hear something coming up exactly where I'd hiked along an animal trail.

I got my bow ready, thinking man, if I get a deer this early, I'll be all set, though disappointed a bit. It would be too easy. Killing the deer wasn't really a sport for me, as I hunted from necessity and my family would eat on it all winter—the sport was in the tracking and in not getting myself lost.

OK, so there I was, hiding behind a pretty good-sized pine at the break of dawn, barely light enough to see where I was at, when something was coming up the trail where I had just walked.

The more I thought about it, this kind of bothered me, because animals have very keen senses of smell and will seldom go where you just went, they go the opposite way. And that meant it was probably a grizzly bear, the one creature out there not afraid of humans. And that was the last thing I wanted to meet up with. The thought that one is adequately armed with a bow against a grizzly isn't much of a thought.

I reached for my bear spray, the one thing I always carried any time I was in grizzly country. I pulled it out of my belt holster and got it ready. No point in even messing around with my bow, that would just make it mad.

I held my breath as this thing got closer and closer and bigger and bigger sounding. Holy crap, from the sound of it, this was one big bear. It was breaking the timber as it came along and making all kinds of noise, a kind of huffing sound, like it was mad. Oh man, that was scaring me bad, and I even toyed with running, which you never do around bears.

I waited it out, as that was all I could do. But just as it got to what sounded like about 50 feet away, it turned and took off running, making an even louder crashing sound. I could hear it thumping along and it really sounded huge. And that's when it dawned on me that this thing was running on two legs, not four.

I breathed a sigh of relief—the bear must have caught my scent, realized how close I was, and headed out. I right then and there was ready to call it a day and get back to my truck, because one thing I won't mess around with is grizzlies. Well, there are now two things, as you'll see.

As I stood there, waiting for my legs to stop shaking so I could walk on back, here came a big buck running madly through the trees in the direction from where the bear had just gone. I mean, it was scared out of its senses, as it came right next to me. I hated to shoot it, it didn't seem like a fair fight, but I thought of how much venison we'd have through the winter, so I drew back and let go.

I'm a good shot, but nobody could've missed at that close range. I shot it right through the heart and it dropped instantly. I always prided myself on a quick kill, as I hated to see an animal suffer.

So, there lay this big four-point buck literally at my feet. I would have to dress it there and carry it out in several trips, as it was big and no way could I drag it out. So, I set to it, wondering if that grizzly would come back.

I worked quickly, and soon was on my way, carrying part of the animal over my shoulder. I wanted to get out fast, and I was even toying with the idea of not going back for the rest. It had dawned on me that a big buck like that wouldn't normally be that afraid of a grizzly bear.

I got down to my pickup and put the meat into the back, pulling a big canvas tarp over it. I sat there for a bit, wondering if I should go back for the rest. The pickup was parked at the very end of the road, a sort of staging place for hikers and horseback riders at the trailhead. I was the only one there, and I didn't expect to see anyone else, given the time of year it was and that it was hunting season.

I got out my little camp stove and made myself a cup of coffee, then set there some more. The sun was now moving up and lighting the high timber, so I figured it was about 7 a.m. I had all day to get the rest of that buck out.

I sat there for the longest time. I sure didn't want to meet up with that grizzly. I decided to leave several times, then would think of all that meat and would change my mind. I finally decided the best way to do something was to do it, and I got up and hiked back up there.

Man, was I on edge. That bear had sounded like several bears all wrapped up into one, and I sure didn't want to meet it. As I got close to my deer, I kind of stealthily snuck up, thinking it could be there eating on it. I watched real carefully for some time before going on in and putting the second load over my shoulder and heading back down. The only thing around was a bunch of ravens, and they were making a ruckus. I knew they wanted to eat some of that deer.

I stopped several times on the way back to make sure I wasn't being followed. I had heard plenty of stories growing up about bears taking a hunter's kill, though not directly from them. But there was a first for everything—which I soon learned.

I got back to the truck and removed the tarp and put the second load in the back. I could get the remainder in one more load.

I once again toyed with the idea of just heading out, pretty happy I had managed to get a nice big buck that fast, especially after hearing that bear. I got into the truck and sat there for a minute, kind of getting my breath and enjoying the woods, knowing I wouldn't be back until next year.

Once again, I was indecisive. We needed the meat, but I sure was getting tired. It took an hour every time I hiked back up there. I didn't want to go again. I was tired and admittedly, still spooked.

That's when I noticed the ravens again—they seemed to have followed me out. There was a good dozen or so sitting in the trees above, looking down at me and silently watching.

I decided to go get the rest of the buck. It would be enough to get us through the winter. I had three kids and a wife to think of, and I didn't make all that much doing construction. I had already got our wood in for the winter, and this would make sure we got through OK. I made sure the tarp was covering the meat so the birds couldn't get it, then I headed back up the hill.

Once again, I was extremely cautious, but once again, there was nothing around. I retrieved the rest of the buck with no problems, other than being pretty tired at that point. I noticed there were no ravens around, which surprised me. I figured they would be trying to munch on what I'd left there. I decided they must all be down at my truck. I hurried down, happy to be getting off the mountain with my last load. It would be a successful hunt. I could go home and have a nice hot dinner with my family.

I was nearly back when I thought I heard something. I stopped, trying to figure it out. It was in the distance, in the direction of my truck, and sounded like a hundred ravens all cawing at once. It was kind of unsettling, to be honest. I had never heard such a ruckus, and it made me wonder, as I'd been in the woods since I was a kid.

It got louder the closer I got to the trailhead, and I finally had to put the deer down and stop. What the hell? What in the world was going on? The only way I can describe it is that it sounded like a football game with ravens cheering, instead of people, but once in awhile I could hear a howling that for sure wasn't any raven.

I knew enough to not just blunder back to my truck—I don't think anyone would have been that stupid with something like that going on, although I know some people who think humans are the top of the food chain and don't worry about anything.

So, I left the deer and kind of skulked through the trees, dodging and hiding until I came close enough to see what was going on. As I finally got to where I could see my truck, I thought I was imagining things.

There was a big bunch of ravens flying and swooping around my truck, probably thirty or more, all squawking and making loud raven noises, diving in when they dared for a bite of the feast. The deer portions were no longer in the bed of my truck, but had been dragged a few feet away and were on the ground, scattered around into various pieces. What had done the dragging? And tearing?

I knew that ravens and wolves had a symbiotic relationship in the wild, as ravens will tell wolves where the prey is by making a lot of noise, but they need the wolves to kill it. A raven can't even get into a carcass without something big tearing it up first. What had these ravens attracted to my deer with all their noise?

Now, I could see something huge over behind the truck, all bent over. At first I thought it was the grizzly I'd almost met earlier and a chill came over me. How could I get to my truck and get out of there? What if it stayed there a long time, guarding its feast? How could I get back?

But now the creature stood up. Holy crap! This was no bear! I felt my knees literally get weak, and I thought I might pass out. I could only see it from the chest up, as it was behind the truck, but what I saw was the legendary creature called Bigfoot, and I can tell you, the rest of it was big enough to go with the feet. It had a chest as thick as any grizzly or even a Kodiak Bear, and it stood taller. It had dark reddish hair all smooth in spots and rough in others, and the hair on its head was longer. Its head seemed to have a sort of crest on the top, where the forehead met the upper skull, and it had huge piercing eyes—eyes that seemed to see me.

I suddenly felt sheer terror like I've never felt before or since, even earlier when I thought a huge grizzly was coming right up the trail towards me. It was almost a supernatural terror, like I was looking at a creature from another reality, though I knew it shared my world, as it was eating my deer. But it felt like I was looking at a combination of legend, reality, and imagination.

But I knew it had sensed my presence somehow, it knew I was there, watching, even though I was well hid. It stood straight up and walked around the back of the truck, and then I could see it had a big chunk of meat in its human-like hands and had black fingernails. It paused a moment, carefully placed the meat on the truck bumper, then started coming towards me. The ravens went into a frenzy, diving for the meat.

I was frozen for a moment, just watching it coming, noting how huge its stride was, how muscular it was, how long its arms hung, as if watching a movie, very detached. But then something kicked in, a flight instinct, and I turned and started running. I ran for my life, and I knew I didn't have a chance, as that creature could move so much faster than me with its long muscular legs.

I ran right to the rest of the deer I'd been carrying, jumped it, and continued on. I then kind of turned towards the road, as I knew instinctively to somehow try to parallel it if I wanted to get back and not get lost. It was a good six or seven miles down to the main road.

I could hear this thing coming after me, and it started screeching like a banshee, only ten times as loud. It sounded really mad. It was breaking tree branches as it came, and then, all of a sudden, it stopped.

I knew it had found the rest of the deer, and it apparently found that more interesting than chasing me. It had succeeded in getting me out of its territory, and I hoped it would consider that good enough, but I kept running. I could feel my heart beating hard, and I knew it was from a pure deep animal fear. I thought of that poor buck I'd shot.

I soon cut out of the trees and onto the road, where I could make better time, and I ran and ran, my mind focusing only on getting back to my wife and kids.

I eventually came to the main road, but there was no traffic, so I kept running. It was a good 20 miles back to town, but I was tired when I started, and I was rapidly losing strength.

After a few more miles, I had to walk, and I kept thinking I could hear it coming behind me, but it wasn't there when I looked. I was afraid to turn away, and I started walking backwards, nearly tripping numerous times. I was depleted, I had nothing left, virtually no energy. Finally, I tumbled to the ground. I had hit the wall.

I just lay there, and then came the sobbing. I was traumatized and couldn't help it, but it seemed to be cathartic to cry. But now I noticed it was starting to get on towards evening. I had to get out. It was too cold to spend the night out, and I wasn't sure if the beast wasn't still coming after me. It could eat its dinner, take a nice long nap, and still catch up to me.

I managed to stand up and start slowly walking out, but it was a supreme effort. I felt like I had just climbed a huge mountain, and I realized I hadn't eaten since breakfast, nor had anything to drink. And I had climbed that mountain three times and run a good ten or so miles.

Just as I felt like I couldn't take one more step, a car came down the road. I managed to flag it down, though I thought for awhile it wasn't going to stop. It was a woman from town, and she acted half afraid of me, but I finally convinced her to call the sheriff to come get me.

I remember feeling the deepest sense of desolation as I saw her tail lights going on down that road into the deepening evening, but it wasn't long before a pickup came by and stopped. It was a local, and he gave me a ride.

I told the local guy my truck had broke down, and by the time we saw the sheriff coming down the road, I had decided I didn't want to tell the story to anyone, as I knew they would think I was nuts. So, we flagged him down, and I lied and said my truck wouldn't start. The sheriff offered to take me out there, but I said I'd get it tomorrow, and the local guy gave me a ride on home.

I didn't go out there for several days, but finally my brother and I went. My truck sat just as I'd left it. There was nothing there to corroborate any of my story, no deer hide, nothing. I was beginning to think nobody would believe me—even my own brother seemed kind of skeptical, like he thought it had been a grizzly.

But when I got home, I was taking the tarp from the back of the truck, and that's when I realized my bow and arrows were gone. Normally, they would be the first thing I looked for, but I was still pretty out of it. I told my brother, and he just shook his head and looked at me kind of funny. He said someone had obviously been out there and stolen my bow.

But I knew better. Maybe the Bigfoot had watched me shoot the deer and was going to become a bowhunter. Maybe he's out there practicing right now, using that tree I was hiding behind. I don't know, but after that day, I'll believe about anything, and I also believe I'm never going back out there, in fact, I know that as a true fact.

[5] Play Ball!

*We were sitting around a campfire high in that wild coun-
try near Steamboat Lake and the Mt. Zirkel Wilderness Area in
Colorado when this story came along. The guy telling it was a
surgeon, and he told it with such lack of pretense and seriousness
that I knew it was true. But how many times does a kid get to
play ball with a Bigfoot?* —Rusty

My brother Shawn and I were kids when this happened—I
was ten and he was eight. That makes it about 30 years ago.
Time sure flies, because it seems a lot more recent.

It all started with my parents getting a divorce. They
hadn't been getting along for years, but were staying together for my brother and me. When they started throwing
things at each other and breaking stuff, I think they realized it was time to part ways.

My dad had a full-time job, so we stayed with my mom.
Mom didn't want us hanging around alone while Dad
worked, and he was out of town a lot. He was a trucker.
Mom had a small business making nice gourmet specialty

soaps, which she could do anywhere. She sold them at local shops.

All this meant moving, since Mom couldn't afford the
little bungalow we were renting. Dad kept it, and we could
go stay with him whenever we wanted, which was good.

So, my mom called up family, and we moved back to
her hometown, which was about 30 miles from where we'd
been living. She was getting child support from Dad, but
she still didn't have a lot of money. So, we moved into a
free house, the one built by my great-grandparents. It had
been sitting empty for 20 years or more.

I'm kind of struggling with telling this, because it brings
back some hard memories. My dad ended up getting killed
in a trucking accident a few months after we moved. I think
the majority of their fighting had to do with money, as well
as him being gone all the time, and if things had been a
little better, they wouldn't have split, and who knows, my
dad might still be around, though I would never have had
this experience. But life is what it is.

My great-grandparents' old house sat on the side of a
huge hill—some might call it a mountain—right above a
big sandstone cliff, with outcroppings also right above it. It
was about eight miles from town, which meant we'd have
to ride the bus once school started. And the dirt road up
to the house was no picnic, it wound around up the side of
the hill. We were the only ones on it, it ended at our house,
so in the winter, we'd be responsible for keeping it open
and plowed. Mom told us it was a temporary place until we
could get on our feet, hopefully before school started.

My great-grandparents had homesteaded the place,
and they'd owned quite a bit of land there. I don't know

how many acres, because it went right up to BLM land, and none of it was fenced. It had been their cattle ranch, and they had built the house. It was really cool, made of sandstone blocks they'd quarried right out of the nearby cliffs. It sat on the only level place on the mountain, a big meadow with a spring next to the house, which was obviously why they chose that site.

It was really an awesome setting, no neighbors and nothing but wilderness as far as you could see. We're talking about northern Idaho.

It took a lot of work to get the house ready. We all pitched in with the cleaning, and that was bad, as there had been mice living there. But at least it was stone, which meant once it was clean, there was nothing in the walls to worry about. We washed windows and cleaned the wood floors, made of pine from higher up on the mountain.

My dad helped, and when it was done, it was really neat. Unfortunately, there was no indoor plumbing and we had to use an old outhouse—that got old pretty fast—and shower in an outdoor shower we built. But the rest of the place was actually kind of magical—an old barn and an old chicken coop and even some old farm equipment. And my mom loved the beautiful wild roses that had grown all around the house, and there were even a few remnant iris from when my great-grandparents lived there.

We finally were able to move in, and at first it was just the thing for two young boys with nothing much to do on a summer day. We spent our days exploring, though Mom wouldn't let us go into the trees, as she was afraid we'd get lost. But we didn't really want to anyway, as they seemed kind of dark and spooky.

Mom was doing her best to make the place a home for us, and she at first spent a lot of time cooking and baking and making it seem real homey. She would also make her soaps, which were made of goats milk and different natural scents, like lavender and peppermint. They were really nice, and she could sell them as fast as she could make them. We would help her a lot with that, but that was about the only chore we had to do around there.

We soon grew to love that old place. I can't tell you how many adventures we had there, mostly in our own imaginations. Except at the end, and those were real—too real.

Well, all went well at first. Did I mention we really loved that place? At least, we boys did, and in retrospect, I know it was just a lot of hard work for my mom, trying to deal with life with no running water and way out in the middle of nowhere. But Shawn and I were free spirits, running and exploring and living like wild animals. We especially liked to play softball—until the ball disappeared, that is.

About our third month there, it all came to a screeching halt. Our carefree lives became lives of fear.

It all started when Shawn and I were playing on a rock outcropping. I don't recall exactly what we were playing, but I remember he was standing at the very top of it, a sort of sandstone hoodoo, when he just stopped as if frozen. Knowing us, we were pretending to be climbers or pirates or something and were making a lot of noise.

But Shawn just stood there, staring into the trees that edged the big meadow the house sat in. The treeline was maybe 50 feet from us, and the forest very thick and dark. Shawn was literally frozen.

At first I thought it was part of the game, so I just waited for him to say "Ahoy matey" or something and inform me he'd just spotted some enemy of some sort who we now had to vanquish. But he didn't, he just stood there, and after a bit, I began to think he really was looking at something that was scaring him. My first thought was a bear or mountain lion or maybe even a moose.

I finally asked him what was up, and that seemed to break the spell. He came down off those rocks as fast as he could and started running top speed for the house. I didn't know what he was scared of, but if he was that scared, I figured I'd better run, too, so I followed.

He came barreling into the front door and slammed it behind us and locked it. Mom had gone into town, making a soap delivery and getting groceries, so we were on our own. Shawnie looked like he'd seen a ghost, and he went all around the house, locking the doors and windows. When I could finally get him settled down enough to talk, he told me he'd seen a huge man standing back in the trees a bit, watching us. I couldn't see it because I was too low.

I asked him why that was so scary, as I really didn't understand it. Maybe it was a sheepherder from across the mountain or something, but why would it be so scary? He said he didn't know and couldn't explain it, but it was the scariest thing he'd ever seen. If we'd had a phone, he would've called Mom to come home.

Well, he went and sat on his bed in his bedroom, and I kind of looked out the curtains a bit, going around from window to window in the house, trying to see if the man had come closer. I didn't see a thing. But when we heard Mom drive up, Shawnie started crying, saying it was going to get her. So I went outside and helped her carry the groceries in, keeping an eye out and trying to explain to her what was going on.

She went into Shawn's room and talked to him for a long time, and when she came out, I could tell she was just a little spooked herself. She went outside to look around, and I couldn't stand the thought of her going alone, so I followed her. We looked all around the house and, even though we couldn't see far up to the trees, we stood there and looked for a long time.

Shawn and I both were kind of known for having wild imaginations, so I think my mom didn't really believe there was anything there, and I'm not sure I did. Maybe he'd seen a deer or something and made it into a big man. Shawnie had an imaginary friend at one time, so we kind of wondered.

Finally, after dinner, Mom sat down and we all talked a bit. Shawnie told us it couldn't be a bear because it had a human face, but it looked all hairy. He swore he was telling the truth and that he had actually seen this thing, and he asked if we could all leave right now and go to Grandma and Grandpa's house, at least for the night.

The poor guy was scared to death. Seeing this pretty much convinced me he was telling the truth, and I think Mom was now wondering if there hadn't really been something there.

It was late, but seeing how upset Shawnie was, Mom decided it would be OK to go into town for the night, so off we went. It wasn't quite dark when we left, and I remember her locking the house up, something she never did before.

In my mind, it seemed kind of desolate looking as we drove off.

Well, we ended up staying several days, and even at that Shawnie didn't want to go back. But we had to, we couldn't move in with Grams and Gramps, they didn't have enough room, as my Uncle Jim was already living there, having just been laid off his diesel mechanic job. So we returned, and everything was just as it was before at the house, nothing was different.

This event really traumatized Shawnie, as he refused to go outside to play anymore, even though it was the height of summer. I had to walk with him to the outhouse. All he wanted to do was stay indoors and make models or draw or read, and he always kept the doors locked.

That of course put a damper on my outdoor activities too, as I sure didn't feel comfortable without him, and with nobody to play with, I might as well stay indoors, too.

It wasn't long before he started having nightmares. He always dreamed the same thing—someone was trying to unlatch his window and get in. He would wake up to a scratching noise and fly out of his bed and into Mom's bedroom. After a few nights of this, he refused to sleep in his room.

Since I hadn't heard anything, I just figured he was dreaming it all. So, Mom moved his little single bed into her room, and he slept in there. She was really getting worried about him, and asked me what to do, but I had no idea. Shawnie was now wanting to go live with Dad.

Finally, Mom conceded, and sent Shawnie to live with her parents, as Dad was never home. It was supposed to be a short stay until Shawnie got over this phobia he'd developed or whatever it was.

He would have to sleep on their couch, but they lived in town, so no more wondering what was in the trees. When Shawnie left, he said he was really scared for me and Mom and felt guilty for leaving us and wanted us to get out of there, too.

Well, I really missed Shawnie and hoped he'd get better soon. Mom was usually around, but when she went into town I would sometimes stay out at the house alone. It was really boring to ride all over the place with her, delivering soaps, and she always had to visit with whoever she saw.

The first time I stayed alone there, I have to admit I was pretty spooked. Shawnie had made me promise to not go outside, but I still wasn't real sure he'd really seen anything, and I missed being outdoors a lot. I stayed inside the first few times, except for the outhouse part, which scared me to death, I admit. But at least is was on the opposite side of the house from the forest and not too far.

Finally, I could stand it no longer. I needed to go outside. I couldn't live indoors any more, even though Shawnie had said if I went out, I might never come back in.

Well, I went out. I walked around the outside of the house and strained to see into the forest, but I didn't see a thing. I then got a little braver and walked over to the spring. The spring had a small fence around it to keep cattle out, with a gate.

There, inside the fence, right next to the spring, was the softball that had been missing for a few weeks, since before Shawnie saw the man. I wondered how it got there. We had been playing ball on the opposite side of the house, and no, we hadn't lobbed it over the roof. This was really odd. We always set it on the back porch when we were done with it, and one day, it was just gone.

What I saw next about made my heart stop—huge tracks in the mud, and they had five toes. I mean, these things were big. OK, I went back inside, forcing myself to walk and not run, then I locked all the doors and windows.

When Mom came home, she wasn't real happy with what I'd seen. We went to the spring. She took a bunch of photos. Then we left and went into town, where she told Gramps. We all came back together, including my Uncle Jim. They went over to the spring and looked around a bunch. Then they asked me where we had been when Shawnie saw the thing, so I pointed it out, and they went over there.

When they came back, they looked real grim. They had found more of the big tracks over there in the soft duff, though they looked older. Everyone was beginning to believe Shawnie. My mom looked very serious.

I know Mom would've left then if she would've had anywhere else to go. But we stayed, although we were now extra cautious. It wouldn't be long before the rancher who leased the land would bring up his cattle to eat the tall blue-stem grasses. When fall came, he would move them back into the lower meadows. But soon he would be around some. Mom swore we would be out of there by the time he moved his cattle out.

So, the summer wore on, and I was now pretty much never left alone. The rancher moved his cattle in, and they were now all around, grazing on the tall grasses. I liked that, because I knew they would be like a warning system, alerting us if something were around.

Then the bad news came. Dad had been killed in a wreck. Someone had swerved in front of his truck, and rather than hitting them, he'd gone off the side down a steep embankment. It was all over for him.

This hit Mom really really hard. Not only did she have to deal with her own grief, but she had to deal with ours, plus taking care of all his personal stuff, as he had no close relatives. The only good thing was that he had a life-insurance policy that would pay for me and Shawnie to go to college, as well as money for my mom.

Now Mom was never at the house, and I grew tired of it, as she made me go everywhere with her. I would go stay with Grams and Gramps when I could, and it was good to see Shawnie, who seemed to be getting back to normal, but there just wasn't enough room there.

So, I persuaded Mom to let me stay home one day. The rancher was coming around a lot, and I promised I'd stay inside, so she relented. I think by now she was both physically and emotionally exhausted.

I fiddled around indoors a bunch, then really wanted to go outside. I'd promised not to, but I wanted to go see if the softball was still there at the spring. I was still wondering how it got there.

Mom had made a batch of blueberry muffins, so I grabbed one, carefully looked around, then started out. It was then that I saw movement in the trees right above the spring, and I put on the brakes as fast as I could. Before I could even turn around, something black stepped out of the trees and leaned over the fence around the spring. It picked up something, then stepped back and started slowly coming my way.

My brain said it was a bear, though my instincts said otherwise, but I'd always been told to never run from a bear. So, I started backing down to the house, all the time watching this thing. It slowly walked towards me, and all of a sudden I felt a blackness go into my heart. I knew I was going to die. I shouldn't have broken my promise. I should've stayed inside.

People have asked me what it looked like, and all I can say is that it was bigger and more muscular than the biggest football played I've ever seen. It had longish hair, and it really wasn't apelike, nor was it human, but it was kind of like both but neither.

It's hard to describe, but if you ever see one, you'll have its image burned into your brain forever. I've tried sketching it, but I'm not much of an artist and it doesn't work. For some reason, maybe because of its playfulness, I got the impression it wasn't that old, maybe like a human teenager.

Anyway, I was finally back to the house, bumping into it backwards. Now, if I could just inch my way around to the door, I'd be OK. The black creature stopped as if it knew what I was thinking and that I would soon be gone. It raised its arm and threw something to me. I say to me and not at me, because it was a gentle toss, a perfect toss, and the softball practically landed in my hand without me doing a thing to catch it.

I stood there, kind of stunned. All of a sudden, I knew it wouldn't harm me. I didn't even pause, I just tossed the ball back to it. It must have seen Shawnie and I playing ball.

I couldn't believe what I was doing. I swear I could see a bit of its teeth showing, as if it were smiling, and it then tossed the ball back to me. We both stood there for a long time, and then I kind of came to my senses. I needed to get inside.

I still had the muffin in my other hand, totally forgotten, and instead of the ball, I threw the muffin and ran. I was quickly inside, where I locked the door. I then looked out the window, and it was still standing there. I kind of imagined it felt hurt.

Was this true? How could I possibly know what this creature was feeling? It probably wanted to eat me, deep down inside, and the ball playing had been a lure. But I somehow knew that wasn't what it wanted.

I went into the kitchen and got the bowl with Mom's blueberry muffins. I stepped outside and around the corner of the house. The black creature was still standing there. I threw the whole thing at it, bowl and all, then ran like heck. Once inside, I could see it picking up the muffins and eating them. Even though I was scared stiff, I actually started laughing. Finally, it turned and went back into the trees. I then heard the sound of an engine. It was the rancher.

Oh man, now I realized what I'd done. I'd thought for a moment it was Mom, and she was going to bust me for eating all the muffins. Times were hard, and that was our snack food for the week.

I had never baked anything in my life, but I soon found her recipe box and was making more muffins. I finally had them in the oven, and by the way they smelled, I had done something right. I was about to take them out when I noticed a shadow over the window, then a huge black face looking in. I screamed as loud as a ten-year-old boy can scream. It ducked and disappeared.

The rancher was soon at the door, knocking and asking if I was OK. His name was Mr. Richfield. I was in shock, and told him what had happened. He ran outside and looked all around, but saw nothing. I think he thought I was making it all up, as he hadn't been in on the recent happenings.

By now, the muffins were burning. I managed to get them out of the oven, and they weren't too bad. I have no idea how I had the presence of mind to deal with that, but I let them cool and put them in another bowl like the one I'd thrown outside.

And just in time, as Mom was coming up the road. Mr. Richfield met her outside, and I could see them talking for a long time. Then they both came into the house. I offered the rancher and Mom each a nice warm muffin. Mom didn't even notice they were warm and a bit overdone. We all sat down and talked about the Bigfoot, but no way was I going to tell them I'd played ball with it and fed it muffins. They would think I was crazy either way—for doing it or for pretending I had.

But now, having seen it up close, I wanted nothing more to do with it. I wanted to be far far away, with Shawnie, in town.

Mr. Richfield was very concerned for his cattle, as they were now milling around, though I could tell he was having trouble with the concept of a Bigfoot being around, or even existing, for that matter. He was going to start carrying his rifle. I think he was kind of shook up when Mom pulled out the pictures of the footprints. He was more shook up when they went to the spring and found fresh ones.

Mom asked him to stay around for a bit while she packed a few of our things in a duffle bag. It was nearly dusk when we left, and Mr. Richfield was right behind us going out. As we wound down the road, I knew we would never come back, not to stay, anyway. We would get our stuff out and the house would sit there, abandoned again. It made me feel glad to be leaving, and yet kind of sad.

As we wound down the road, I turned and waved good-bye out the open window, hoping the Bigfoot would find the muffins I'd left for him by the back door, along with the softball.

[6] The Peeping Bigfoot

Katie had been on several of my flyfishing trips, and she had never said one word around the campfire. She always just sat there and listened. She was kind of a spitfire, so it always surprised me how quiet she would get. But she was a member of Sisters on the Fly, so I figured she got all her talking done when she was exclusively around other women. Then one night, she told this story and had us all scratching our heads in amazement.

Was it true? Had she really witnessed and actually held in her hands the most amazing proof of Bigfoot and then voluntarily let it go? If so, I admired her for what she did, but if not, I admired her for her good storytelling skills. But the way she told this, the earnestness and seriousness, made me think she was telling the truth. As with all my stories, I change the names and usually the places and retell them with permission. I guess only Katie knows if this really happened, as well as the Bigfoot in the story. —Rusty

I had been somewhat avoiding my friend Kelly for some time, as she had recently broken up with her long-term boyfriend, and it seemed every conversation we had de-

volved into a counseling session, with me being the coun-
sellor. Given my own propensities towards disastrous rela-
tionships, I didn't feel all that qualified to advise anyone, so
for me, the simplest solution became avoidance.

But Kelly finally caught up with me, and she had a pro-
posal I couldn't turn down—free housing in exchange for
helping her with her resort house. Kelly had a place in the
small tourist town of Teasdale, near Capitol Reef National
Park in southern Utah, and she wanted to leave and go on
a long trip, driving around the West pulling her little trailer
in an attempt at making a new start, exploring new places
and trying to grasp the concept that there are lots of fish in
the sea when it comes to other people. She was a very de-
pendent type person, and I thought the trip would be good
for her.

Since I had recently sold my own house due to financial
difficulties, I was becoming desperate for a place to live,
which I hadn't anticipated would be so hard. But having
two dogs was making things impossible when it came to
renting.

I soon found myself on the road to Kelly's, even though
it was a long drive and I really didn't want to leave my
hometown. At least I was going to a beautiful place. I had
spent many good days exploring Capitol Reef National
Park once, but I didn't know the town of Teasdale all that
well, except having driven around it a few times. It was a
very pretty place—very pastoral with old stone houses, big
cottonwood trees, lots of green fields, and a pioneer feel to
it.

I was kind of dreading meeting Kelly, as I knew I was in
for it as far as having to listen to her bemoaning her lot in

life regarding men and about everything in general. I had tried to plan it so I would get there not long before she left.

I know that sounds cold, but I'd already spent many hours on the phone with her, and I was beginning to realize there was nothing I could do or say, it all had to come from within her.

I arrived at her house just as a huge black storm hit the national park behind me, right where I'd come through not minutes before. I had watched it coming from a long ways off and tried to high-tail it through the park so as to not get caught in a flashflood. I knew it hit hard because Kelly called me later and told me the flooding was ready to come over the highway. She described it as quite a sight, and she was almost ready to turn around, but managed to make it through.

Oh man, I would've been hurting if she'd turned around, cause I would've had to spend the night listening to her talk about how everything in life was against her. As it was, she left me a three page document outlining every little thing she wanted done, most of it involving things I hadn't signed up for, like painting the inside of the house. I was beginning to feel exploited, and decided to just ignore the note. I hadn't told her I would do the maintenance, only the guest part, which was enough, checking people in and cleaning up after them.

Kelly's place was really beautiful, an historic two-story cut-stone house which she'd decorated with old-time stuff. It had a lot of character. But the real beauty was in the extensive gardens she'd created on the five acres of land around it.

Man, what a lot of work. No wonder she wanted to take off, maybe her ex wasn't the only reason she needed to get away. There was no way I could keep up with all the gardening, and I had told her so, but her note included all the gardening things she wanted done.

After she left, I walked around a bit, my jaw hanging open. It just went on and on—hollyhock gardens, rose gardens, stone pathways under huge black locust trees, lilacs, small irrigation ditches everywhere with rustic redrock bridges across them, lots of shady nooks and crannies, and one path that led to an old blue-and-white 50s trailer hidden in some big willows, the kind that's shaped like the canned ham you buy for Christmas dinner.

I then decided to tour the house, as she had guests coming that same day and I would need to know where things were. The house was really cool, very old-fashioned, with old magazines and Zane Gray books and Navajo rugs and lace curtains—and a big deck that looked out over a big green lawn and Boulder Mountain in the distance with its volcanic cliffs. What a paradise. Why would she want to leave this? The human mind can create traps for us no matter where we are, I guess.

I then decided to check out what would be my quarters, a small and very cozy cabin that Kelly called her art studio. It had a neat wood-burning stove, a very tiny shower, and a tiny kitchen with a bright red sink and room to barely turn around. It was modest, but cozy with a nice little rock patio under yet more big locust trees. It set on the edge of the property, away from the main house, and right smack on the edge of wilderness. I could see long yellow fields of dried native grasses that stretched to the flanks of Boulder

Mountain, with nary a sign of civilization between the cottage and what appeared to be many many miles of nothingness.

That cabin was the original house on the property and was over a hundred years old, Kelly had told me. It had a very rustic feel to it, and I really liked it.

The dogs loved the place. They could run all around the five acres, as it was all fenced, and they loved the irrigation ditches. They explored and played while I moved my stuff in, such that it was, just my sleeping bag and a few clothes and some odds and ends like my little espresso machine and some towels. The dogs were soon in the cabin, sleeping on the cool stone floor, wet and totally worn out. I think they were pretty happy.

The guests showed up around mid-afternoon, a couple from California. They seemed nice enough. They'd come to spend some time hiking in the national park and were very excited. I checked them in and didn't see them again after that.

The first night was pretty awful. I was supposed to sleep on the couch, but it was hard as a rock. I tossed and turned for an hour or so before I decided perseverance wasn't going to make things any better, so I then went out to my pickup and got my camping cot. I set it up and promptly went to sleep. The bad night continued—around 2 a.m., the legs on my cot collapsed. This was a bit of a shock, to say the least. One of the legs had just snapped off. I tried to fix it, but it was cheap metal and there was no way.

Now what? I couldn't sleep on the floor, as my back needed something softer. The couch had been bad enough.

I was bummed out, to say the least, and kind of mad at Kelly for not telling me about the poor sleeping accommodations, as I could've bought a small mattress. I just sat there, wondering what to do.

I had left the door open when I went out to get my cot, and had locked the screen door when I came back in, enjoying the cool fresh air. Teasdale sits at somewhere around 7,000 feet elevation, and I'd been down in the hot desert some 2,000 feet lower, so the cool air was nice.

I sat there on the couch, tired and bummed out and experiencing that array of emotions that goes with being sleep-deprived and having a problem you're not sure how to solve.

It was then I heard something softly crunching through the leaves. It was early-August, but the area was having a huge aphid infestation, and all the big black locust leaves were turning yellow and falling from the trees, all from the aphids, just as if it were autumn. There were clouds of the tiny insects everywhere, and also tons of Lady Bugs and their larvae eating the aphids.

So, now the ground had a layer of dead leaves, and I could hear something walking towards the cottage. Probably a deer, I thought, but just then the dogs started growling. Not like them to growl at deer, they usually would want to go out to chase them. This wasn't a deer.

I heard the footsteps stop, as if whatever it was had just heard the dogs. Now the dogs were growling, looking at the screen door, ruffs standing high on their backs. I'd never seen them like this, and it spooked me. I got up and closed the door and locked it. I was afraid to even look out to see what it might be.

The cottage had no curtains, which it didn't need because of its isolation. Earlier, while lying there falling asleep, I had looked out at the stars and thought how cool it was to see stars while indoors, but now I wished I could close everything off from the outside. Tomorrow, I'd get sheets from the main house and hang them over the windows. For the time being, I'd have to hope there was nothing out there, but I knew better.

I don't remember much after that except waking up at dawn kind of curled up on the couch, stiff and sore and very tired. A wasp had somehow gotten into the room and was flying around looking for a way out. I opened the door and kind of herded it out, noting the sun hadn't quite come over the distant red cliffs yet. It must be about 6 a.m.

I then looked out and noticed a sort of path coming up to the cabin from the edge of the property. It looked like something had kind of dragged its feet through the leaves, as it was a wide path, not like where someone had carefully walked. It came right up to the front door and stopped, then it looked like it went back the same way. That was puzzling to me—what had it been? Was this what I'd heard last night?

I kind of stumbled around, took a brief shower, made some coffee, fed the dogs, then went out and looked around some more. It seemed like there was a strange smell back where the leaves had been dragged through, although fading. Maybe a skunk had visited. I let the dogs out, and they immediately ran back and started sniffing around, then started growling again. This wasn't anything I'd ever seen them do before. They then kind of high-tailed it back into the cabin, acting scared.

I got everyone into my pickup and went into town for some breakfast, as I didn't have much around to eat. I ended up at the one and only little breakfast cafe, where I got a bagel with cream cheese. I sat there for a bit, people watching, though there weren't many to watch. A couple sat down next to me and started talking in kind of a hushed tone, yet I could still hear what they were saying.

They were talking about a Peeping Tom in town and said that several people had seen him and it seemed people were suspecting who it was and how he should be arrested and all that. Small-town talk, although it struck me as odd that anyone would want to be a Peeping Tom in a town as well-armed as most little rural Utah towns seemed to be. I wondered if that was who had visited me. After awhile, the couple left, and so did I.

The first thing I did when I got back was go into the main house and get some sheets for the cabin windows. The guests had already left for the day, so I didn't get to ask them if they'd heard anything. Probably for the best, as I didn't want to alarm them.

I covered the windows, then searched around in my truck and found my canister of bear spray. I'd bought it when camping in Montana the previous summer. If a Peeping Tom came to my door, he'd get a face full of pepper spray. I kind of hoped he would, to be honest, cause I was pretty mad. I value my privacy.

That night, nothing unusual happened, but I was glad for the curtains, as it was now a full moon and very light outside.

The next day, I did what was becoming a routine—go into town and get a bagel and people watch. Nobody was talking about Peeping Toms, but there was plenty of other talk—someone had backed their car into someone else's fence, that sort of thing. This was such a small town, maybe all of a hundred people, that it seemed strange to me that anyone would want to wander around and spy—it seemed like you could learn everything you wanted to know by just sitting in the coffee shop.

But I found out later that whoever was spying, at least one of the spies, wasn't trying to learn about people.

That night, whoever it was returned. It was again about 2 a.m., and the dogs woke me, once again growling. They were very quiet, though, as if trying to alert me while laying low, as if they were afraid they'd be discovered and were in danger. In fact, they both ended up hiding in the bathroom, good guard dogs that they are.

I awoke instantly, and I could hear something scratching along the wall, just outside the main part of the cabin, where I was now sleeping on a futon mattress from the main house. The guests had left, their vacation being over.

This was a very small cabin, and I was sleeping in the main room, only a few feet from the door, which had a dog door in it, the kind with a clear plastic flap that opened when pushed on and then clicked back into place using magnets. It was really bright outside, and the light from the full moon lit up the flap.

I was just laying there, wondering what was going on and reaching for my bear spray, when I could see something come up next to the flap, blocking the light—something dark, like someone wearing black pants—and someone with thick heavy legs. They just stood there, on the other side of the door, and I could easily have pushed the dog door open and touched them.

OK, to say I was scared would be an understatement. Before, I had heard something, but now I could actually see it.

Now I could hear the what-ever-it-was move a bit and stop at the window. I knew it was hoping to see in but couldn't. The dogs were now hiding in the little bathroom, and I was about to join them, when I heard a low moaning sound. It was unearthly, there's really no way to describe it.

I ran into the bathroom with the dogs and locked the door. If this person or thing did get into the cabin, they would have one more barrier before they could get us. I was terrified, and the dogs were shaking like leaves.

I then came a bit to my senses, ran back into the main room and grabbed my cell phone and dialed 911, whispering to the dispatcher. She said someone would be there soon. I knew her definition of soon wasn't the same as mine, as it would depend on what part of the county the deputy was in—and it was a big county.

Much to my surprise, I heard someone drive up in just a few minutes. I then heard something running around the house, and they slammed their hand or something hard against the bathroom wall as they went by.

Soon, a deputy was knocking on the door. I described what had happened, and he said this was becoming a regular thing for him. He wanted badly to catch this guy and considered a Peeping Tom a big waste of his time. In fact, I was the third call tonight.

He went outside and shined his light around, then said he was going to go drive around. By now, it was about 3 a.m., and I couldn't go back to sleep. I was OK when the deputy was there, but as soon as he left I became terrified again. I grabbed a few clothes, some dog food, and jumped into the pickup, taking the dogs with me and locking the house behind me.

I didn't have anywhere to go, but I knew I couldn't stay in the cabin. What if it came back? I was beginning to think it wasn't human after hearing that howl. It was beyond me as to what it could be, all I knew was that it was big and black and had a heavy raspy voice.

It takes about two minutes to drive through Teasdale. I passed all the sleepy houses, most with their porch lights on to deter the Peeping Tom. The town looked surreal in the moonlight, and the big white sandstone ridge above town glowed.

I came around the corner off Center Street and that's when I spotted him! There was the Peeping Tom, looking into a window. I immediately dialed 911 again.

The guy saw me and took off running in the opposite direction. Well, here came the deputy, driving up and down the streets, looking with his big spotlight. But the guy was long gone.

I was really shook up, as my sense of security was gone. I didn't want to go home, so I drove to the nearby town of Torrey, just a few miles down the road. I felt safer in a different place.

It was nearly dawn, so I just kept driving, as nothing in Torrey was open. I turned onto the highway that goes towards Boulder Mountain and then intersects a back road to Teasdale. I really didn't want to go home, but I had nowhere else to go, so I turned and began slowly driving on this back road, called the Teasdale Road. It cuts through an area that has few houses and, for the most part, goes through ranch fields and occasional wild areas of pinyon forest.

I was driving slow, trying to delay the return home, hoping it would be dawn by the time I got back. It was now really dark, as the moon had set.

I couldn't figure out why I was still so scared, as it didn't make sense. The Peeping Tom was long gone, so there was nothing to fear.

I came to a place where the highway was kind of squeezed between a hillside and a rocky cliff, surrounded by trees and very dark, and just then, I saw it! Two red glowing eyes on the highway directly in front of me, maybe only 50 feet ahead!

I slammed on my brakes and knew I was going to hit it, but just as I was almost upon this thing, it stepped aside. I knew then exactly what it was I was looking at, even though I had never believed anyone who told me they'd seen one—it was a Bigfoot. My pickup lights illuminated it from head to toe, and there was absolutely no mistaking it.

The creature was well over six feet tall and was really broad shouldered, but not deep chested. I did notice its arms were way longer than they should be, hanging down past its knees. And its large eyes glowed a strange reddish-amber color in the truck lights.

I had the presence of mind to hit the accelerator after it got out of the way, and I suddenly went from a near stop to peeling out. Just as I went past it, it reached out and whacked my pickup, then let out a deep-throated howl.

The dogs were on the floor, whining, and the engine was revving, but I still could hear the cry it made—and it was just like the sound I heard at my door earlier that night, only much louder. It made me actually start shaking with fear.

It was a miracle I could even drive, but I kept accelerating. I looked behind and saw those amber eyes—it was chasing me!

I was going about 45 when I finally lost it.

I was several miles from home, but I was so shook up I had no intention of going back to the cabin, as this thing knew where I lived. It was probably as surprised to see me as I was to see it on that back road, but I knew it had been at my house and would come back. And it wouldn't take long to get there at that pace.

I was beside myself—where could I go now? I again drove through Teasdale and on out to the main highway and back to Torrey, having made a big loop. Dawn was now on the horizon.

I drove up next to the bookstore, which was in an old house with a long drive down to it from the main road that was next to an open field. There was nobody around, so I slipped out of my PJs and into my clothes and let the dogs out for a bit. They were still scared stiff, but I coaxed them out for a few minutes. I tried to give them breakfast, but they wouldn't eat.

It then occurred to me to call the deputy, which I did. I told him what had happened, and he got real quiet. He told me he was going off shift, but asked if he could come over in the evening and talk to me. I said yes, but I had no intention of spending another night there.

The Torrey cafe was now open, so I went in and had breakfast and drank lots of coffee, trying to decide what to do. I then went out and just sat there, again trying to decide what to do. I had promised Kelly I would manage her place, but I knew I couldn't stay another night. But new guests were coming that afternoon, and I had nowhere else to go. I was in a quandary. Maybe I should check them in and get a motel room.

So, I then went to a small motel and rented a room for the night. Torrey is near a national park, so the prices are expensive, but I could manage for one night, and that might give me time to figure out what to do.

I then called Kelly. She didn't answer, so I left a message to call me. She was on the West Coast, and it was much earlier there, so she was probably still in bed.

I felt lost, with no place to go, but I finally went on back to the cabin. I needed to get things ready for the next guests.

Eventually, the night's fears seemed to dissipate. I went into the main house and tidied a few things and lit some scented candles, made some cinnamon rolls, and did a few things like that.

But then I went back to the cabin and started packing things up. I had to leave, there was no question about it.

As I went out in the back to water some flowers, that's when I saw it—a huge track in the wet garden soil. I stood there for a long time, holding my breath, then went inside and locked the door. The fear was back. I could barely make myself stay. I just wanted to flee.

The guests were now arriving. I gave them my cell number so they could call me if they needed anything. I hated to spoil their vacation, but I felt it was only right to tell them that someone or something had been around and to be cautious and keep the curtains closed. I offered to refund their money if they wanted to leave, but they opted to stay. It was two moms and their three teenagers, and I think the kids found it all really exciting.

It was now late afternoon, and still no callback from Kelly.

The deputy soon drove up, and I took him out back and showed him the footprint. He got plaster from his truck and made a cast of it. He was again very quiet.

He then came in, and we sat there for a bit, talking about last night, and I told him to keep an eye out here, as I was leaving for the night and there were guests. I told him I was too terrified to stay, and I somehow felt this thing was after me for some reason, although I had no idea why.

I headed for the motel in Torrey. I felt comfortable and safe in the motel room, and had soon gone to sleep, even though it couldn't have been past 8 p.m. I was exhausted from no sleep the previous night. I was soon awakened by Kelly.

She was beside herself when I told her what had happened and that I was leaving. As predicted, she tried to intimidate me into staying, and when that didn't work, manipulate me, then shame me by saying I had made a deal. Yes, I had, but it hadn't included being threatened by Bigfoot and Peeping Toms. I wasn't getting paid enough for this, I told her, but she missed the irony, which was that I wasn't being paid at all.

I told her I would stay until these guests left, but she needed to head home. She didn't have anyone booked for another week, so she had time. At this point, my own emotional and physical safety took precedence over everything.

I was laying there, thinking about all the psychological techniques Kelly was capable of, and not in a good way, when the guests at the house called.

There was something messing around at the little cabin. They really couldn't make out what it was, but it seemed to be really intent on getting inside, and they were scared.

I dialed 911. I was getting to be a regular customer. They said the deputy was on his way.

After an hour or so, the deputy called me. Whatever it was had torn off the screen door. The guests were leaving and getting a motel room. I guess the kids didn't think being scared was so much fun after all. For some reason, the Bigfoot really wanted inside the cabin.

The next day, I went back and packed all my stuff into my pickup. The guests came back, and I refunded their money. I guess it had been a really terrifying night with this thing banging around and moaning, and they'd been scared to death. They were glad to be out of there. I would soon be, too, and I couldn't wait, even though I had no idea where to go.

I locked up the cabin and went back into the main house to try to figure out what to do next. I was sitting there when I remembered my shampoo was still in the cabin, so I went back over for it.

As I was walking back out, I just happened to look up into the rafters. I had never noticed there was something hanging up there, as you could only see up there when in the bathroom, as that's where the attic entrance was. A sense that something was wrong hit me like a ton of bricks. I wanted to get the hell out of there, to run away, but I somehow knew I had to see what this was.

I got out the little stepladder and stood on it, looking up into the attic. I couldn't quite make out what was there. I then climbed and pulled myself up. I inched my way over to what looked like a big buffalo head hanging on a timber.

As I got to where I could actually make it out, I stood in shock. My jaw hit the floor. I thought I must be dreaming— and I was very disturbed by what I saw.

It was what could only be described as a Bigfoot skull. It was huge, and it had an elongated crest on its forehead and somewhat of a point on the top. It was covered with a thick layer of dust. I knew there had never been any kind of tangible evidence of a Bigfoot, and I knew I was now looking at proof of its existence. The skull would be worth a fortune.

I didn't want to touch it, but I carefully lifted it from the big hook it was hanging on. It was heavy, and the bone had an especially thick textured feel to it. I carefully slipped back down with it and out into the main room. In the light, it was even more terrifying. Its eye sockets were huge, and it had smooth yellow teeth, much like those of a human, except much larger.

This was a true treasure—this was the real deal. I set it on the kitchen table and just stood there, shocked. I knew this skull could make me a wealthy person, but I now felt I knew why the Bigfoot was coming around. This skull had the means to not only make me rich, but to possibly turn the world of the Bigfoot upside-down. It was proof of its existence. I thought of taking photos of it, but something held me back, some kind of respect for the animal this once was, maybe.

How long the skull had been there, I had no idea. I knew Kelly had owned the property for about five years. Something told me she had no knowledge of this, as she was the type of person who would capitalize on it.

Yes, I was mad at Kelly and no longer considered her my friend, but that had no bearing on what I decided to do next—I was acting on what I knew was ethical and right.

I carefully wrapped the skull in a sheet and set it by the front door. The Bigfoot would be back, I knew that, and I also knew this was why. It would find the skull and leave—it wanted this skull badly, and I couldn't blame it. I would probably never know the logistics behind it nor how the beast knew the skull was here, but it didn't matter. The skull should be returned to the ones who stood to lose if it were ever found.

I was no longer afraid, now that I knew why the Bigfoot was coming around. It wasn't after me at all.

I would stay one more night and see what happened. I decided I would enjoy my last day there, and I went into the main house and made a nice meal and sat and read while the dogs lay around in the shady yard.

It was finally evening, and I decided to go to the cabin. I knew the Bigfoot would be back, but I wasn't as worried about it. I knew it would take the skull and leave. Maybe I would even get another look at it, although what I'd seen the previous night on the Teasdale Road was about enough for one lifetime. But I had lost my fear and become fascinated by these creatures that I hadn't even known existed until now.

I went back to the cabin and sat up for awhile, but soon nodded off. Sure enough, it was 2 a.m. when I woke up—but something was different. The dogs were growling, but not like they had before, but more like a normal growl.

I soon heard footsteps in the dried leaves, and now something was trying to open the door, turning the knob. I somehow knew this was a human, not a Bigfoot. Was this the Peeping Tom? I sure seemed to attract trouble lately.

I dialed 911 and whispered into the phone what was going on, then I got my bear spray and quickly opened the door.

But there was no one there. Instead, I heard a man screaming from down the drive. The Peeping Tom was running away!

Now I could see why he was running and screaming. The Bigfoot was back! Holy crap, that thing was huge! And he was coming for the door, right at me. I slammed the door shut. The dogs let me know it was back—they were in the bathroom, hiding.

I was now terrified. What had I been thinking to stay?

But all was quiet, and I knew the creature had found the skull.

I finally got up the nerve to peek out the window. It was standing there, skull under its arm, looking directly at me. Its reddish-amber eyes glowed, and I felt like they could see right through me. It gave me the creeps, yet I knew it wasn't going to harm me.

I slowly opened the front door a crack, even though I was scared. It seemed like the moment of a lifetime, like the meeting of two species, and I wanted to let it know I understood—exactly what, I don't know, but I understood something—there was something between us.

I wanted it to have the skull. I didn't want proof of its existence. I knew they existed, and that's all that mattered. If others knew, they would hound it and hunt it and who knows what, try to get a body for a museum or something.

It just stood there in the moonlight, and I just stood there in the doorway, until finally I said, "It's yours, big fellow, take it."

I doubt very much if the Bigfoot understood what I'd said, but it turned and walked away, skull held tightly, the long hair on its arms swaying as it walked.

I went back inside and calmed the dogs, and just then the deputy showed up. I told him about the Peeping Tom, who I was sure was long gone by then.

I told him I didn't think we'd be having any more problems with him. When he asked why, I told him the guy had a run-in with a Bigfoot and would probably never go outside again. I'm not so sure he believed me, but I didn't care.

I left the next day. I moved back to my old town, where I found a cheap house to rent and eventually ended up going back to school and studying biology, which I love, and becoming a teacher.

I heard later that indeed the Peeping Tom had ended his crime spree and was never a problem again. Kelly came home, and the Bigfoot never was seen again, as far as I know.

As I drove away that day, I noticed the sun's rays were shining directly into the attic window. I stopped my car on the road for a moment—I could make out the beam where the skull had hung. It was the solution to the mystery of how the Bigfoot knew the skull was there—it had seen it from the road when the moonlight was shining just right.

I drove on and never turned back.

[7] The Crossing

* *

This story makes me wonder if the coyote in it ever got caught and what it did to make a Bigfoot mad. It was told around a campfire near a lake on Grand Mesa in Western Colorado, where a bunch of us were attending a fly-tying seminar, or at least that's what we told our wives. It was actually more of a "let's see who can tell the biggest lie" seminar—and a few beer never hurt when you're trying for that kind of accomplishment. But I never did figure out if this was a wild tale or a true story. —Rusty

My story's kind of short, but it was something I'll never forget—man, I mean never.

My son and I had gone to North Dakota to visit my great aunt, who was in poor health. We also went to check out the possibilities of selling her huge wheat farm, which she had leased out to a farmer for many years. I would inherit it when she died, and that unfortunately didn't look to be very far away.

The trip itself was kind of sad and stressful, so on the way back, I wanted to show my son, Teddy, some sights and unwind a bit. Teddy was 14 at the time, and he still talks about what we saw. We both sometimes ask each other if we really saw it. I'm glad he was there as a witness, or I might think I was going insane or hallucinating.

On the way home, we went through South Dakota, and we decided to go see, among other things, Mount Rushmore, which frankly was a bit disappointing to me—just some guys' heads carved into a granite cliff. We later went to see the huge carving of Chief Crazy Horse, which was much more interesting and artistic. But that's just me.

Anyway, not far from Rushmore is Custer State Park. This is all in the Black Hills, and boy, are they pretty. I'm from Nevada, and when I saw the Black Hills, I just wanted to move there. I later took my wife, Sue, there for a month-long camping trip after Teddy went off to college. We really enjoyed that, but I have to say I was kind of nervous after dark, especially after what Teddy and I saw.

But back to the story, what there is of it.

Teddy and I were driving along one of the scenic drives at Custer State Park (I believe it was the Wildlife Loop Road, appropriately enough), watching for wildlife. The kind of wildlife we saw we never anticipated and will never forget.

The park has a herd of about 1300 wild bison, known as buffalo to most of us. We were driving along through the beautiful ponderosa forest when we came to a huge meadow, and it was filled with buffalo. I bet there were a good 500 there, grazing.

I stopped the car and we set by the edge of the road, along with other tourists, watching these massive animals. They are truly big and scary, which we saw first-hand with a small group grazing right next to the road. We were too afraid to get out, but a few other people were standing by their cars taking photos, candidates for Darwin Awards, I guess.

All of a sudden I noticed something at the forest's edge, not too far from us, about a third of the way around the side of the meadow. I pointed it out to Teddy, and we got out the binoculars to see what it was.

It was a coyote, and it was pacing back and forth along the edge of the trees. I thought this was kind of unusual, and we talked a bit about what might be going on, when all of a sudden the coyote made a break and shot out into the middle of the buffalo, kind of going through a break in the herd. It was trying to get across the meadow, and didn't want to skirt it because of all the people everywhere by the roadside. Its only choice was to go right through the herd.

That coyote was one brave animal, and you could tell it was scared to death. It kind of just put its head down and ran along, until a big bull buffalo started after it, then it high-tailed it into an even faster run. I was worried we were going to see it stomped, something I didn't care to see, yet alone have my son witness, but it eventually made it across.

I remarked to Teddy that the coyote must have really pressing business to risk its life like that, running through a herd of buffalo. That's when he grabbed my arm and pointed me back towards the side of the meadow the coyote had come from.

Something big was coming through the trees, and it was making a lot of noise—tree limbs crashing as well as an angry bellowing sound that filled the valley. Everyone that had been watching the coyote turned to see what was making the ruckus, and it was only a matter of seconds before everyone had gotten back into their cars, some of them peeling out and leaving as fast as they could.

Keep in mind that this was in broad daylight, early afternoon, and there were at least 20 other witnesses.

We thought we were seeing a bear coming through, a really big bear, but it was running on its hind legs, which was weird. Bears can run fast, but on all fours. Their center of gravity isn't meant for sustained upright motion. And this thing was fast, I mean fast.

It came barreling out of the trees and right smack into that buffalo herd, not a bit worried about being gored or stomped. It was chasing that coyote, and why I will never know. Let's hope for the coyote's sake it never caught it.

I don't know how tall a buffalo stands, but they're big, and this creature was even bigger. It dwarfed the buffalo. Unlike the coyote, it wasn't afraid and went straight through the herd, and if anyone got in its way, it just pushed it aside. Can you imagine pushing a 2,000 pound bison aside? It actually even knocked one big bull to the ground.

When the buffalo realized what was coming, man, they scattered to either side, squealing in fear. What in heck would scare a buffalo like that? Buffalo really only have one natural enemy, and that's humans, but they have to be armed humans or the buffalo will make mincemeat out of them.

Teddy had grabbed onto my arm and wouldn't let go. I kind of had to peel his fingers from my jacket when it was all over.

He was watching through the binoculars with his other hand, and he then handed them to me. The look on his face was pure shock. I took the binocs and glassed this thing as it was running along, and since we were at kind of an oblique angle to it, I could see its face, even though it was almost all the way across the big meadow.

It was the stuff of nightmares, let me tell you that. A huge head coming to a kind of point, huge eyes, huge muscles, long arms, a very efficient running gait that looked like it could run forever and not get tired, and hair—not fur, but hair drooping off its long arms, and shorter hair elsewhere. But what really got to me was the face—it was human. Not almost human, but flat-out human, kind of like someone in a drawing of early humankind in Africa. Very sentient and very intelligent.

It was soon gone into the trees on the other side of the meadow, and the buffalo at this point had started stampeding right towards the road—a massive black whirlwind—right where we and a dozen other cars were.

This Bigfoot thing or whatever it was, was damn scary, but having a herd of buffalo stampeding your direction was even scarier—though different kinds of scary. The Bigfoot still comes to my dreams in sort of a horrific way, but the buffalo stampeding brings out a sweat when I think of it.

I'm telling you, we humans are totally sheltered. This incident made me think of the early Pleistocene humans and what it must've been like to live around dire wolves and saber-tooth tigers and such. Not fun.

Well, we were already in our car, so when I realized what was happening, I gunned out onto the highway and drove like hell and got away from there. Everyone else followed my example, and it didn't look like anyone was caught.

I think I'll end this story here, as telling it always makes me shake a bit, and sitting around this campfire at the edge of the woods doesn't help much. I know there aren't any buffalo around here, but I'm not so sure about Bigfoot. I'm glad I brought my RV, and anyone who feels like I do about sleeping in a tent is welcome to sleep on the couch. Or maybe you can have my bed, as I'll probably be sitting up all night after telling this.

[8] The Good Samaritan

· ·

We hear lots of stories of Bigfoot eating wild pigs and deer and occasionally even people's pets, so this story was a nice change from all that. It kind of reminds me of a story told in my first book ("Bigfoot Campfire Stories") about a guy who rescues a dog, although this one has things turned around a bit. In any case, it's nice to know that some Bigfoot care about other animals.

This story was told by a retired physics professor during a fishing trip on the Gunnison River in Colorado. He was a kind and soft-spoken guy named Ed who always released his catch whether he was required to or not. I really liked him, and we stay in touch and occasionally get together when we're in the same neighborhood, as he now lives in Colorado. —Rusty

I was living in Arizona at the time of this story, in my mind one of the most unlikely places to ever even think of Bigfoot, yet alone see one. It was in Prescott, so maybe there's enough forested areas around there for them to live, but Bigfoot was a new concept for me, I can tell you that.

We had a nice place on the edge of town, right in the ponderosa pines, with a big deck that went halfway around the house. It was a nice spot. My wife and I have since retired and moved back to Colorado, where we're originally from.

Well, one day I was sitting on the deck when I spotted something out of the corner of my eye back in the trees. At the time, a cougar had been coming around, so I was pretty aware of movement. The cougar had actually dragged a dog from its yard, although the owner had managed to scare it off and rescue the dog, but just barely.

So, I was just sitting there, drinking my morning coffee, thinking about some stuff at work (I was a college professor) and half asleep, when I saw this movement back in the trees.

I'm not one to defy nature, so I got up and went inside. If it was a cougar, I wasn't taking any chances. I also wanted to grab my camera and see if I could get a good shot of one, if that's what it was.

So, I was running into the kitchen, where I'd put my camera on the table, and then running back around to the living room, where I'd been sitting outside on the deck, when I saw something for sure out the window, but it appeared to now be running away from the house, only maybe 30 feet from the deck. Had it come up to the house? If so, how did it turn around and retreat that dang fast? I couldn't believe it.

It looked like the tail-end of something huge, but I only got a glimpse before it was back in the pines. It was dark brown, except for the bottoms of its feet, which, as it picked them up running, I could see were lighter in color. It had really wide shoulders, like someone wearing shoulder pads would have.

I did have the presence of mind to take a photo, which I later showed to my daughter, who's a semi-pro photographer, and she was pretty shook up. Like all Bigfoot photos, it wasn't real definitive, just a black blurry object, but given the story that with went it, it was proof enough for me.

As this thing ran away, I was standing there in shock, and I could actually hear the timber breaking as it ran through, crushing branches and all. And man, it was fast as a greased pig (which I've never seen, but I hear are fast).

So, I just stood there for a bit, then it dawned on me to go outside and see if there were any tracks or anything. I was scared to death, but it had obviously run away, so I figured I would just look around a bit and stay close to the house. Maybe I could get some good photos, if there were prints. It would make people more likely to believe me.

I'll be darned if I opened the door and almost stepped on something! I was shocked! It was a little kitten, maybe about two months old, huddled there, a gray-and-white long-haired tabby cat with the cutest little lynx-like face.

I stood there for a minute, wondering where it had come from and why it didn't run away, when I noticed it was twisted all weird. It then started meowing this tiny little meow and trying to stand up. It could pull itself up with its front paws, but its rear-end just dragged along behind it. It was injured, and maybe pretty seriously.

Oh jeez, what the heck, where did this little thing come from? Was there some relationship to this and what I swear looked like a Bigfoot? There had to be—it was no coincidence, and the kitten had to be carried and put there, no way could it move itself. I'd been sitting there just moments ago, so even if it did manage to drag itself up onto the porch, I would've noticed it. Did the Bigfoot injure it? Was it trying to get help for the kitten?

I went inside and got a small towel and carefully kind of rolled the kitten onto the towel and then very gently wrapped it up and took it inside. I offered it some water, and it was very thirsty. I didn't want to feed it, as I knew it would maybe need surgery right away, so I found a small box and made it a little bed in it and headed for the car. The kitten stank to high heaven, a strong odor of skunk or something really rancid.

As I went outside, that same odor floated through the air. I can tell you, this really gave me pause. Truthfully, I was scared to even walk out to my car.

As I drove down the lane and out to the highway, I dialed my vet and told them I was on my way. Since I have two dogs (golden retrievers, both with my wife that day), I knew the vet.

I quickly got the kitten there, where they examined it and said they needed to take X-rays to see what was wrong, but they suspected a broken pelvis. OK by me, I would figure out the bill later. You can't let creatures suffer.

It wasn't long until the vet came out into the waiting room and confirmed a broken pelvis. And on top of that, the little guy had a partially crushed hip joint. The vet said the pelvis couldn't be repaired, but it would heal naturally if we kept the kitten restricted, but they could repair the joint. The vet also wondered why the cat smelled so bad. Of course, I wasn't sure then, although I know now.

I said goodbye to the little fellow and went home, knowing it was in capable hands. But before I left, they asked me what his name was, so I just off the cuff came up with Charlie. So Charlie it was.

They did the surgery the next day, then called me in the afternoon to tell me Charlie was doing well, but they wanted to keep him for a few days and make sure he would be OK.

In the meantime, my wife, Carrie, came home and I told her all about it. By then, I had loaded the photo of the Bigfoot onto my computer. She didn't like this story one bit, and I could tell she was both scared and incredulous, but I just didn't know what to say. Like most of my life, I was just a passenger on the bus.

Carrie had gotten where she wouldn't let the dogs go outside without standing there watching them, even though we had a fenced yard, and I figured that was a good idea, given that the cougar had tried to carry off a dog not too far away.

But now Carrie was even more nervous, and I have to admit I was, too. I made sure all the doors were locked, then had to kind of laugh at myself. What I'd seen leaving the yard, well, no lock on earth would stop that beast.

That night, I swear I could hear something talking to me, and it woke me up. I just lay there, really still and quiet, and I could hear it again—a voice saying something in a language I didn't speak. It was coming from the deck, and it seemed like it was sad, although why I felt that, I have no idea.

Shoots, was I terrified. Carrie was still asleep, but the dogs were under the bed, growling, but really quietly, like they didn't want anyone to know where they were, like you would if you were hiding from a predator and yet trying to be defensive. That confirmed that I wasn't dreaming.

I lay there a bit, then decided I had to go see what it was. My family's safety was my responsibility. I'm not a hunter, so I didn't have any kind of weapons, but I went anyway. Maybe I did it for my own sanity, I don't know.

I didn't turn on any lights, I just very softly crept into the living room, keeping along the near wall where I could sort of sneak up to the window and look out onto the deck. Believe me, I felt nothing like a hero, which is what you're supposed to be when you do something brave while you're scared to death. I felt more like a fool. The dogs, brave as they are, stayed under the bed.

I very quietly looked out onto the deck, but there was nothing there. The voice was gone, and I was beginning to think it was all a dream, but I could feel my hands shaking.

I finally got the courage to turn on the deck lights, and that's when I saw it. Something was on the deck. It kind of looked like a basket. My first thought was oh no, not another kitten.

I knew it was utterly stupid to open the door and go out there, but I had to see what it was. Maybe it was some kind of bait and I would be a goner as soon as I stepped out, but I went anyway.

The first thing I noticed was that smell again. It was so powerful it nearly knocked me over. I slowly stepped out to where the basket thing was and picked it up. I expected to be attacked by something, but wasn't. I didn't want to take it inside, as it really stank, but I wanted to see it better, so I stepped into the living room and turned on the light.

It was indeed a basket, though a rough one, one made perhaps by large hands that couldn't really do fine work. It looked like it was made from dried sumac, and inside it was a dead fish, a smelly dead fish, maybe a small carp. The combination of the dead fish and the skunky smell almost made me throw up.

Now Carrie was up, coming into the living room, asking what was going on. I didn't say a word, and when she saw the basket and dead fish, she got really quiet.

"Let's put it in the basement for now," she said, "Where we can't smell it. Wrap it in plastic."

"Why not back outside?" I asked.

"It's a gift. We don't want to refuse it."

"A gift?"

"From the Bigfoot."

Needless to say, neither of us got any sleep. We sat in the dark and listened for weird noises, scared to death, but we also talked quietly about the whole situation. Why did the Bigfoot bring the kitten to us? Carrie was convinced it was being a good Samaritan and saving it. I wasn't so sure. I know I just wanted to go get a motel room and never come back, at least not at night. This whole thing was getting really weird.

The next day, I called the vet to check on Charlie. He was doing great, but of course it was too soon for him to come home. I then asked what they thought would cause an injury like that. Had Charlie possibly been mishandled by something big?

I think the vet thought my question was a bit strange, but he answered that it was without doubt caused by getting run over. A car had run over Charlie. It was a very common injury when cars and cats met.

I pondered this a bit and shared it with Carrie when she got home from work. She was now even more convinced the Bigfoot had found Charlie and brought him to us for help and then brought us a gift in thanks. I found it hard to believe we were even having that conversation. I pride myself on having a scientific bent. A few days ago neither of us even believed in Bigfoot, especially not one in Arizona, and now we were talking about Bigfoot Samaritans. How quickly things change.

The next night, all was quiet, although at one point I heard the dogs growling, but only for a moment. Carrie and I kind of huddled together all night long, neither of us getting much sleep. We were terrified, and our house was no longer our refuge. I was actually wishing I'd seen a cougar instead of a Bigfoot.

The next day, I went to the university and Carrie went to work, leaving the dogs locked in the house for the day, the doggie door closed. I ran home between classes and let them out.

Finally, the next day, it was time for Charlie to come home. My wife had bought a small cat carrier and picked him up after work, as I was too busy. I hated to see what the vet bill was, but it actually was pretty reasonable, and Charlie's prognosis was good.

Since he was so young, he would heal fine, but we had to keep him confined for several months so his pelvis could heal. He could hang around the house with us, but for short stretches only at first, and the rest of the time he was to be in this big metal carrier they loaned us.

Carrie set the carrier up in the living room, where Charlie could see us and be part of the family. We fed him and took turns holding him while the little guy purred. He sure was cute, but when we left him for the night, he meowed and meowed. I wanted to bring him into the bedroom, but the dogs wouldn't leave him alone, they kept trying to sniff him, scaring him, so we left him in the living room. He finally settled down.

That night, someone (or something) tried to break into the house. The door into the living room was pushed open, breaking the lock. The dogs at first went ballistic, then they bravely headed for their refuge under the bed. Carrie and I both ran out into the living room, and we must have scared whatever it was off.

We called the sheriff. I thought about our actions later, and we must have lost our minds, as a burglar could have easily shot us. I guess we both were thinking about animals getting in, like a cougar, and were brave because of Charlie. We didn't want anything to happen to him. We moved him into our bedroom after that.

Two deputies showed up and checked everything out, but found nothing. They did both remark on a strong smell outside. They took photos, looked around a bunch, then eventually left.

I asked Carrie why they didn't fingerprint the broken doorknob. Her reply was, "It's a good thing they didn't, as they wouldn't know how to deal with Bigfoot fingerprints."

Carrie had the theory that the Bigfoot was checking to see what had happened to Charlie, but I thought maybe he had come back to get him. Either way was bad, we sure didn't need a Bigfoot coming around, gift or no gift.

In the meantime, my daughter, the photographer, had developed an interest in Bigfoot and had done a lot of reading on the internet about other people's sightings and experiences. She said all we needed to do to keep it away was to put up a game cam or some kind of surveillance camera, and we would never see it again. I thought this was kind of funny, but I did go get one. It didn't stop it one bit, but later, my daughter said I had failed to hook it up to a recording device, so no Bigfoot video.

Carrie said we needed to show the Bigfoot somehow that Charlie was fine, and then it would go away. Maybe it had heard the kitten meowing that night and was worried. I was beginning to wonder how she had developed such an insight into these creatures, but maybe it was woman's intuition.

So we took to sitting on the deck, holding Charlie and letting him drag himself around a bit each evening, as the vet said this would help develop his muscles. And I swear if more than once I didn't get the feeling that we were being watched. It made my hands go clammy.

I was actually toying with the idea of selling the house and moving into town, though I didn't mention it to Carrie. I found out later she was thinking the same thing. But after that, the beast didn't try to break into the house again, although it did continue to leave gifts on the deck—rocks and sticks and another dead fish.

Eventually, Charlie recovered, and he's now a magnificent and most gorgeous cat who rules the roost, including the dogs—though goldens are pretty easy to rule over, they're so mellow. We spent many hours out on the deck and then in the yard rehabilitating Charlie, and I know the Bigfoot was there for some of that time, watching from the forest. I could always tell, as I would just get this strange feeling of being watched. It always gave me the creeps, and I never got used to it. I was always scared to death of that thing.

As Charlie recovered, the Bigfoot visits became less frequent until the creature finally quit coming around. We not too long thereafter retired and moved to Colorado, getting a place in town with a big yard where Charlie can play all he wants.

But while we were in Prescott, Charlie was never allowed outside alone—it was too dangerous, with cougars, coyotes, and...well, I almost said Bigfoot, but I guess that would be wrong, since that particular Bigfoot saved Charlie's life.

Thanks, Mr. Bigfoot, wherever you are, you were a true Samaritan.

And the basket? It never lost the odor, so we eventually threw it away. Carrie took it to a dumpster in town, as she didn't want the Bigfoot to know and thus hurt its feelings. But now we both wish we'd kept it—how often does one get a handmade sumac Bigfoot basket?

[9] Ride Alone No More

· ·

Some stories are so heart-breaking that you almost wish you'd never heard them. This one was told by a retired fellow who lived in Albuquerque and was up fishing with us near Steamboat Springs. He told it to me in private after the trip over a beer at a local pub. It pretty much made me want to cry.
—Rusty

I don't tell this story very often, as it makes me feel bad— and rightly so, as I often wonder how things would've been if Jamie hadn't disappeared. I miss him, and I know he would've been there for me through all these years. I wish I had been there for him when he most needed me.

But I'm getting ahead of myself here.

Jamie was my older brother by three years. I was 12 and he was 15 when this took place. My grandparents owned the Circle Bar Ranch in northeastern Oregon, over by the Wallowa Mountains, although it's long since been sold and divided several times. But they put a lot into that ranch, and my dad grew up there, along with his two brothers. My dad inherited it, and he sold it after this happened, and it went into other hands.

Jamie's disappearance had everything to do with him selling it, as my dad had originally wanted to be a rancher all his life. But after that, none of us wanted to ride alone no more.

Jamie and I grew up ranching, it was our family way of life. We had a trailer out next to my grandparent's big ranch house, as did my dad's two brothers and their families. It was a big extended family, and it was a great way to grow up. We had cousins all over the place to play with and do things with when we were little.

But then my dad's one brother finally left, as ranching was getting harder and harder to make a living at, and he got a good job with a trucking company, and he and his family moved into town. Eventually the other brother also left, as he messed up his back and couldn't do hard work any more, so he took a desk job with the county.

That left us as the only ones still interested in ranching—me, my mom and dad, and Jamie. We pretty much ran things at that point, as Gramma was stoved up with arthritis and Grampa was winding down from too many years of hard work. I often wish my dad had moved us all into town like his brothers did their families.

That's a bit of backstory, so I'll now get to what happened. It was fall, the time we rounded up the cattle from the high country and brought them down to the ranch fields for winter. It was a time we all looked forward to, as the roundup was hard work but exciting, and we loved autumn up in the timber. All the leaves were changing and the air was crisp. We would see lots of wildlife, and Jamie and I got to be real cowboys, which we thought was cool.

My dad would load the horses into the stock trailer, and my mom would pull a little camp trailer, and we'd head up into the mountains where we had our grazing rights. We'd set up a little camp and use that as our headquarters. Then we'd all go out riding each morning, looking for cattle, then bring them back to a makeshift corral we'd built from logs. Once we got a load, we'd haul them down to the ranch in the stock trailer. We did this until we got them all, and it usually took a week or so, as it was sometimes hard finding them. A few of the old-time cows were onto us and purposely would hide out with their calves, making things difficult.

Jamie and I had helped with the round-up since we were practically babies. One of my earliest memories is of riding in the saddle in front of my dad and crying, him holding onto me as the horse trotted down the road. He thought this was funny, which brings me to what I think was the root reason for what happened.

My mom and dad had some hellacious arguments over their differing philosophies of parenting styles. My dad hadn't been coddled as a child—just the opposite—and he expected his sons to be like him. He was hard on us, and my mom objected to this more than once. And I really think if Dad would have listened to Jamie instead of telling him to not be scared of his imagination, nothing would've happened because Jamie wouldn't have ridden alone that day—my Dad would have been with him.

Me, I listened to Jamie, and I wanted to be out there with him, but I couldn't cause I had dislocated my shoulder and couldn't even sit in the saddle. Mom and I did our best to convince Dad that Jamie shouldn't be out there alone, and Dad agreed, and then he just let him ride alone anyway. I know later he was sorry about that, because he told me so until the day he passed away. My dad was a changed man after what happened, I can tell you that.

So, we were out on the fall roundup, and it was about the fifth day out when Jamie came back into camp a bit early, and he had only a couple of cows. Dad and I were still out, but Mom told me later that Jamie was white as a sheet. He told her something big had been stalking him in the woods, and it wasn't a bear. She never wanted to talk much about it, but I did get her to later describe what he told her, and it sounded to me like a Bigfoot. Remember, we're in Oregon country, and you may not believe in them, but a lot of folks there do—cause they've seen them for themselves.

Jamie and I were no strangers to the Bigfoot concept. We'd seen the Boggy Creek movie and even thought we'd seen one once, but it was too shadowy to be really sure. But that incident left us pretty spooked, though there wasn't much to it.

Of course, Dad thought it was all nonsense. If you couldn't prove it, it didn't exist, was his logic. So, of course Jamie went to Mom, not Dad, with his fears. And Mom wasn't one to discount possibilities—even if she'd never seen something, that didn't mean it wasn't real. She even believed the Loch Ness Monster could be real.

Later, when I got back, Jamie was sitting in the little camp trailer. Mom said I should go talk to him, so I did, and I got the full details. It scared the crap out of me.

Something had been following Jamie around for the past hour before he finally got too scared to continue and came back to camp. He said it was huge and made his hair stand up, and he had a hard time controlling his horse. It just shadowed him through the trees. He wasn't sure what to do, as he knew Dad would laugh at him, but he just wanted to go home now and forget about the roundup.

We were closing in on it, and Jamie was a key player here. For every cow I brought in, he brought in three or four. If he went home, it would prolong everything. Besides, I reminded him, what about me and Dad being out there alone? Dad carried a rifle, but I was unarmed, as was Jamie.

We talked about running away together, then decided it wouldn't be fair to Mom nor Dad. We needed to stick it out, but we needed a plan. So, we decided to ride together from there on out. We knew Dad wouldn't want that, as it would slow things down, so we would pretend we were going our separate ways, then meet up and try to cover both territories.

Mom sometimes rode with Dad, and sometimes stayed in camp and helped him load the cattle. We didn't want her alone and told her so. She agreed that was for the best, and we let her in on the plan of us doubling up so she wouldn't worry so much. She said she agreed, and we should just get this thing over with and get out of there as soon as possible.

I know she told Dad about the Bigfoot, cause he later gave me and Jamie a lecture about bears and how to deal with them (which we'd known since we were little), and he told us he was bringing our rifles back next time he took a load of cattle down. He seemed concerned, but I know he probably laughed when Mom told him it could be a Bigfoot. I'm not sure he ever believed it, to the day he died, in spite of the evidence.

Well, next day, Jamie and I met up outside of camp and rode like wild men, trying to find cattle as quickly as possible. We had twice the territory to cover, since we were riding together. I noted that Jamie kept looking all around him like he was worried, and it was contagious—before long, I was doing it, too. But we didn't see anything but cattle, and we made a pretty good day of it.

That night, I woke up scared. Mom and Dad slept in the camp trailer, but Jamie and I had a big tent we used. Something was outside, snuffling around, and it sounded big. The horses were stomping around in their corral. We always tied our food high in the trees to keep bears and critters out of it, and whatever this was walked over by the food tree. I heard a thump and then silence.

Jamie was terrified. He dragged his sleeping bag over next to mine and whispered to me that he had the same creepy feeling he'd had the day the thing was following him, stalking him through the forest. He knew it was now in camp.

We both just lay there, scared to death, afraid to move. After awhile, we could hear something in the far distance—it was a whoop sound, like this—whawoop, whawoop—with the whoop part drawn out—and you could tell it was made by something large, as it carried a long ways.

Man, were we scared, even though this was far away. But next we heard a reply, the same whooping sound, but this time it wasn't so far away. It sounded like it was just outside the trees around the camp. The ground actually felt like the sound waves were going through it, the call was so deep and loud. I could feel Jamie's arm shaking where he was leaning next to me, and I knew he was beyond scared.

Now the horses were going nuts, like they were trying to break out. Jamie and I both jumped up, too scared to yell for dad, but we stuck our heads out of the tent flap as a light came on in the camp trailer. Dad had a big search light and now he was standing at the door shining it around. This was followed by the sound of his rifle—he was shooting it into the air.

We ran out to the horses and tried to calm them down. If they took off, man, we would never catch up with them. They would go back to the ranch, a good 10 miles away.

Mom and Dad both were soon there, and the horses seemed to be calming down. Dad then looked around camp, shining that big light everywhere, rifle in one hand. Nobody saw anything. After that, we were all too scared to try to sleep. By dawn, everyone was up drinking coffee.

That's when Mom found the tracks. All I can say is they were big, a good 20 inches big, and Dad scowled a bunch while Mom pointed out the toes and the fact that there weren't any claw prints like a bear would leave and that they sank a good two or three inches into the ground, like something really heavy.

It wasn't long until we discovered that our food cache was gone. That was the thump we'd heard—the cache falling to the ground. And the thing in camp had actually untied it. Mom told Dad that you have to have hands to untie something—you know, thumbs. He looked like he was feeling a mixture of anger and fear.

That's when he said he was going back to the ranch to get us all rifles. We weren't to go anywhere until he came back. He gave Mom his rifle, took her pickup, and left.

We were pretty spooked, I can tell you, and we went into the camp trailer and waited for him to get back, which he was in about an hour. He gave Jamie and I our rifles, then said Mom needed to go into town and get more supplies. She didn't want to go, but we needed to eat, so she finally took off after telling Dad not to let us ride alone. He reluctantly agreed.

But he didn't agree to not ride alone himself. That was Dad for you. I think he felt infallible, he had survived so much during his life as a rancher—horse and cattle accidents, bad weather, you name it. And I think he felt like we were all that way—nothing would happen to any of us that we couldn't deal with.

He took off in one direction, and we headed out in another. The roundup was so close to being done, we only had about 30 head to bring in—we could finish soon. This motivated us, and we rode like madmen.

And that was bad, cause it resulted in me getting jerked off my horse as she ran under a branch and dislocating my shoulder. I remember thinking as I hit the ground that it was my own fault and it would come to no good. And I was right. More right than I could have ever guessed.

Jamie caught my horse and helped me get on her and back to camp, where Mom was unloading groceries. She was pretty good at first aid, and the three of us managed to push my shoulder back into place, and man, that hurt. I was just sitting there, tears streaming down my face, when Dad rode in with a bunch of cattle. Jamie helped him corral them while I just sat there, crying.

Dad rode up and just looked at me from up on Mackie, his big sorrel gelding, then asked Jamie where the cattle we'd found were. The two then rode off to get the small herd we'd wrangled up. Mom just stood there. I could tell she was mad. He hadn't even asked what had happened to me.

She gave me some kind of pain killer, then I went into the camp trailer and tried to sleep off the pain. I don't recall anything until the next day, when I woke up in my sleeping bag, my shoulder throbbing. Dad was standing there, looking in the tent flap, asking if I would be OK. He sounded kind of like he felt sorry for me.

I knew Jamie shouldn't be riding alone, and I just assumed he and Dad would ride together that day. Boy, was I wrong. And I know Dad always blamed himself for what happened.

In a way, he should blame himself, but I try to not blame him. He told me Jamie had said he would be OK alone, and they just wanted to get the rest of the cattle and get the hell out. But I can't figure Jamie saying that, after seeing how scared he was. I sometimes wonder if Dad didn't intimidate him in his usual way into saying what he wanted to hear. Mom told me later she thought they were riding together.

It was getting on towards late afternoon, and Dad showed up with his bunch. He said we could be done that day, depending on how many Jamie brought in. There were seven still missing. To say Mom was mad at seeing Dad come in alone would be a severe understatement.

After a bit, Dad got back on Mackie and went out in the general direction Jamie had ridden off. He figured he'd meet up with him and help him bring in the cattle. But Dad never met Jamie. He did find that missing seven and brought them in. I know he was worried about Jamie, but he brought those cattle in.

We were done, as soon as Jamie came in. We could load up the cattle and maybe even get the camp trailer and horses out that evening, if all went well.

It was now wearing on into early evening, and no Jamie. Mom was beside herself with worry. She finally said she was going to go look for him herself, which Dad and I both protested. It finally ended up with the two of them going out while I waited. I sat in the camper with my rifle.

After about a half-hour, I could see someone riding in. The shadows were deepening, so I couldn't make out who it was for a bit, but finally I could see a white blaze, and I knew it was Jamie's little mare, Toots. But to my horror, she had no rider. She was all sweaty and acted like she was terrified—and even though she was overheated and tired, she wouldn't settle down. She wanted in with the other horses. Jamie's rifle was in its scabbard, and that's when I knew he hadn't had a chance.

I put her in the horse corral, managing to take off her saddle and bridle with one hand. I had no way of contacting Mom and Dad to let them know, so I just waited. I didn't want to see Mom's face when she saw Toots. Jamie and I had been close, and I somehow knew he was gone. I was in a kind of shock.

Just as it was almost too dark to see anything, my parents rode in. My mom was always a quiet and kind of stoic woman, and when she saw the little mare in the corral, she didn't say a word. She knew. She just went over to the stock trailer and sat on the bumper and looked out into the forest shadows.

Dad sat down by me and asked if I'd seen or heard anything, but I said no. He got up and went and sat by Mom. There was nothing he could do at this point.

After awhile, he and Mom loaded the remaining cattle, and he drove off, taking them into the darkness and on down to the ranch, where he would also call the sheriff.

Mom and I just sat there together on that bumper, and I put my arm around her and she began to sob. I'll never forget that. But what I'll also never forget is the howling that came out of the trees. It was some distance away, but it was so fierce and angry that we both got up, ready to run for the trailer. It echoed and echoed through the forest.

I was so dismayed I wanted to shout back at it, to scream at it and somehow hurt it, but I knew to keep silent. I didn't want to attract it to us, though I was sure it knew we were there.

Mom and I went into the camper, where we locked the door and sat there with our rifles ready. It wasn't long before a group of men arrived, then another, all driving pickups. It was the sheriff and his posse, a group of volunteers kind of like search and rescue guys. They searched long into the night, but found nothing, and none of them rode alone.

We stayed out there off and on for another two weeks while everyone searched for Jamie, but nothing was found, not a scrap of anything. After that, Dad and I and several friends went out there on our own for weeks searching, but nothing. We always rode together, never alone. When it finally snowed in, we had to give up.

Mom stayed with Dad through the winter, then next spring she left him and went back to stay with her parents in Wyoming. She wanted me to go, but I decided to stay for awhile with Dad. He needed me, and I wanted to go back up in the high country again when the snows melted. I knew I wouldn't find Jamie, but I wanted one last look.

I was afraid to go alone, so Dad went with me. He had sold all the cattle and would soon sell the ranch, so we had no reason to go up there any more, but we both needed closure. We loaded up Mackie and my horse, Buzz, and headed up.

When we got to camp, it all seemed so long ago, and we had both kind of lost our interest in riding, so we left the horses in the trailer and just built a little fire and made some coffee and talked. It was a good talk, though a short one, as the horses were getting restless, and we were getting kind of spooked. It also had started to sprinkle.

Just as we were getting ready to go, Dad went over and picked some wild mountain daisies. He then took them to the place where we had pitched our tent when we were up there last roundup and left them in a little pile. I could tell he was crying, though he tried to hide it.

We got in the pickup and drove off, never to ride again, yet again ride alone.

[10] Lost Lake

* *

*Like the story told by the fellow who had hunted in the
Bridger Mountains, this story also features ravens, but a more
rascally bunch. Those birds put the storyteller in a situation I
would never want to be in, as I'm not as resourceful as he is,
especially with several Sasquatch looking on.*

*I heard this story around a fire in Wyoming, not far from the
Wind River Range, and I'm kind of amazed that Russ, the storyteller, was even out there camping with us, given what he'd seen.
But when I mentioned this, he just laughed and said that the
American Bigfoot wouldn't hurt you. He wasn't so sure about the
Canadian Sasquatch, though, and said he wasn't about to ever be
in the situation to find out, that's why he was in Wyoming. We
all laughed and hoped he was right. Not long after, I received a
case of Lost Lake Ale in the mail. —Rusty*

I'm from British Columbia, Canada, and I can tell you that
Sasquatch is alive and well up there. The stories are plenti-
ful. It seems like anyone who has spent much time in the
outdoors in that area has had at least one or two encoun-

ters. I grew up there, and this story isn't the only one I could tell, but it's definitely the most dramatic.

I grew up in the Bella Coola Valley, and Bella Coola sits on a huge inlet, Queen Charlotte Sound, and we have a lot of coastal weather, even though we're not actually on the coast. It's a wet climate with lots of rain and snow and the huge Coast Mountains towering over you everywhere you go. Mt. Nusatsum is one of the most prominent and reminds me of something you might see in the Himalayas with its pointed massive top.

The people of the Bella Coola region are a pretty self-sufficient bunch, and we're no strangers to wildlife. We even have grizzly bears wandering around, sometimes even in town. Seeing or hearing a Sasquatch up in that country isn't a huge big deal, as a number of people have seen them, although some people don't believe in them. But if they'd been with me, they would for sure.

I'm a bush pilot, though I don't haul people around for pay, but I've been flying in the bush since I was in my twenties. My dad was a pilot, and I guess such things are handed down, as my brother is also a pilot. If you want to get around in British Columbia, flying is the best way to go, as most of the province is wild and rugged with no roads. If you know how to land about anywhere, you have a whole new world opened up to you.

Anyway, this event happened in 1996, quite some time back. I know it was '96 because I had just purchased a used Aviat Husky that year. It was the first and last summer I had it. If you know airplanes, the Husky is every bush pilot's dream airplane. It's similar to a Piper Cub, but can land and take off in literally only a few dozen feet. It's totally amazing. This is partially because it's so lightweight. And part of why it's so lightweight is because the fuselage has a welded steel frame that's covered with cloth.

I had spent quite a fortune on this plane, and I was very very proud of it. It was bright yellow along the bottom half and white on the top. I had toyed with the idea of getting floats put on it, but I didn't want to be restricted to waterways. Anyway, I could land this thing on a short sandbar if I wanted to be on the water, say, for fishing, so I decided to forego the floats. The Husky can get you into places no other plane can go, except maybe a helicopter.

So, having this new (to me) airplane inspired me to get out and see some new country. I decided to go spend several days exploring and fishing some of the lakes near Tweedsmuir Provencial Park. I'd go up to the north section of the park and land on the shores of Nechako Reservoir and do some fishing for cutthroat trout and mountain whitefish. Even though I'd grown up close to that country, I'd never been there. I tried to talk my brother Will into going along, but he had too much work to do.

So, I geared up for a few days out. I was as excited as could be to try out my Husky.

But I never made it to Nechako, as a friend told me it was a bad place to go. He told me the shoreline has a forest of drowned trees and floating debris and there's really no place to land. On top of that, sudden and strong winds funnel down from the Coast Mountains, making landing and taking off hazardous. Of course, this is true about anywhere in that area, but something about the long reservoir channels the winds even worse.

So, I took off from the Bella Coola airport, scouting things out, not sure where I was going. I followed the Chilcotin Highway up over the huge Coast Range, my little Husky bravely climbing like a champ. We locals call the stretch that drops down into the Bella Coola Valley the Hill, but others call it names I can't repeat. It's steep and narrow and scary.

I decided I didn't want to get too far out, the area was too wild and rugged. I soon spotted an intriguing lake that was as blue as could be, that pale milky blue that a lot of Canadian lakes have from glacial till in the water. Glacial till is the soil eroded from glaciers, and it gives the water an unreal color. It's beautiful, but it's also hard on water filters. But I just knew this lake would have some excellent trout, as well as no people. I circled around it and saw no signs of anyone anywhere. It was in a big bowl in the mountains. I would have the place all to myself.

So I thought, anyway.

I found a little sand bar and had no trouble at all landing on it. I had practiced landing and taking off at the airport, but this was the real deal. If I came in too long, I'd be in the lake. I had noticed some logs and such on the sand, but managed to get around those with no trouble. I just sat there for a minute, totally elated. That darn Husky could land as easily as it could take off, needing only thirty feet or so. This little plane was going to take me into places no other human had ever seen, or that I knew of, anyway. I had flown the bush all my life, and never had I been able to land in a spot like this.

I finally got out and walked around a bit. The weather forecast was good, and I had three wonderful days to myself, just me and my little Husky and the wilds of Canada.

I got my gear and started fishing first thing. I just kind of wandered along the lake, hoping to catch something for dinner, as it was now mid-afternoon.

I had soon caught a beautiful cutthroat. I also caught an equally beautiful rainbow trout, which I released. I didn't think this lake had ever been fished by another human. It was about as remote as you could get.

I pitched my little tent not far along the shore from the plane, got settled in, then made a small fire and cooked that trout with a little seasoning and some butter and lemon juice. I added some already cooked pasta I'd picked up at the store, then sat back and ate and felt like I had finally found paradise. This was followed by a beer or two, then I wandered around the plane and took tons of photos of it with the lake and the rugged mountains in the background. I was sure proud of it.

When you're in the north in the summer, it doesn't get dark until really late. I think it was about 11 p.m. when it was finally what I would call sleeping darkness—not really dark, but close enough. I crawled into the little tent and listened to some kind of bird calling in the distance. I noted it seemed unusual to have birds calling at night, but not that unusual. I heard another one answer in the far distance, then I fell asleep.

The next morning I was awake at dawn, ready to go exploring. I made some coffee and had a hot breakfast of eggs and bacon. I love camping out of a plane, as I can carry about anything I want along and don't have to worry too much about animals getting into it.

I then set about getting a small pack ready with lunch stuff and fishing gear. Before long, I was out walking the lake perimeter, which had looked from the air to be about three miles around. I wanted to explore it and check out where the water came from—it looked like it was fed by a good-sized creek that might prove to have some great fishing.

I forgot to tell you what happened first thing when I got up. When I stepped out of my tent, I heard a crack sound that sounded like someone snapping a large branch in two. It seemed to come from around the lake a bit, maybe a few hundred yards away, back in the deep timber. It made me pause, because one has to always be aware of bears. I always carry a rifle, as do most people in the bush.

But what was really weird about this was that every morning, the same thing happened, at exactly the same place. It was like someone was playing a recording. After the third morning of this, I was getting pretty leery, I can tell you that. And those darn birds—every night, the same thing. One would sound off and another would answer from far away, like clockwork, just as I was settling into my tent.

Anyway, I hiked around the lake that first day—or tried to, I should say. When I got to where the creek came in, there was a deep gorge that blocked my passage. I guess it wasn't really a gorge, just a little canyon the water had gouged out—maybe 40 feet deep. So I had to turn around and go back the same way I'd come in. I wasn't able to reach the creek to even try the fishing there, so I went back to camp and fished off the beach again by the plane, and caught another fine trout, who knows, maybe the one I'd caught and released before.

I slept like a baby that night, after the bird calls had stopped. But the next morning, when I exited the tent and heard the crack again, it made me uncomfortable. I felt like something was watching me.

I sat there and had another fine breakfast, but the care-free feeling I'd had the previous day was gone. To be honest, I didn't feel like I was alone any more. I listened for the sound of other people, but heard nothing.

I decided to just kind of hang around camp that day and relax. I would be leaving the next evening, and I wanted to hike around the lake the other direction, but I would do it tomorrow.

I was feeling out of sorts, and not just because of the strange crack noise. I had managed to put on some weight over the previous winter, and the hike the day before had left me a bit messed up. My knees hurt, my feet hurt, my legs were sore, and I was kind of upset with myself. I needed to lose about 30 pounds, and this trip had been the wake-up call. I wasn't as light on my feet as I wanted to be.

I spent the day walking around the lake a bit, fishing, reading, drinking coffee, and just thinking about my life to date. Nothing serious, just planning out the summer and all that. I was 34 years old and wanted to change direction in life. I was tired of my job as a marketing guy for a Bella Coola tourist company—I wanted to get back to doing something I enjoyed. Problem was, I couldn't figure out what.

That night was one of the most awesome and strange nights of my life—in several ways. Number one, I was just drifting off when I noticed something was weird outside, the evening light was different. I slipped out of the tent to the most amazing display of the Aurora Borealis I've ever seen. A huge undulating curtain of purples and reds was draped across the sky as far as the eye could see. I sat and watched it for several hours before I finally crawled back into my tent.

But, as I was climbing out to check out the northern lights, that crack noise went off. It was almost like I triggered it with my arm when I opened the tent flap. I decided it was some sort of warning signal that I was coming out, and who or what was making it had to be watching me and able to see in the dim light, as this time it was dark. That didn't set well with me.

I almost went and slept in the plane, but it would be like sitting in a chair and trying to sleep. It even occurred to me to just take off and leave right then and there, but it was dark and there was no way one could take off that small sandbar in the dark. It was going to be challenging enough in the daylight. And I needed to see where I was in order to circle and climb to avoid the mountains.

When I crawled back into the tent, those damn night birds did their thing again, too. After that, I didn't sleep well at all, and I kept dreaming I was walking around in the thick Bella Coola forests and there were monkeys everywhere. I would wake up, thinking I could hear them chattering, then drift back off again.

The next day, sure enough, that crack sound again when I crawled out of the tent. I was sleep deprived and pretty much ready to leave right then. At that point, I was suspecting I was in Squatch territory and maybe not so welcome. I had never heard of them harming anyone, but I didn't want to be around them, if that's what was going on. After breakfast, I packed up my tent and put everything into the plane. I had decided to leave early, not to wait for evening.

But I just set there for awhile on a big log, looking out at the peaceful lake and thinking about my life back home, and I decided I'd get some fish to take out with me. I would fish for an hour or so, then leave.

I got my fishing gear and slowly began working my way around the lake a bit. It was a beautiful day, and I was beginning to wake up a bit and lose my night fears. I noticed a flock of ravens coming in from the south. They seemed to notice me, as they swooped down and around a bit looking at me, then went on their way. There were about 20 of them. I figured they were youngsters on a lark, as once ravens mate they usually stay in their territory.

I walked a bit and came upon a beautiful little glade at the edge of the deep forest. The forests of this part of B.C. are deep and thick and hard to navigate, with lots of understory. The rains in the Coast Mountains are enough that it's more like a rainforest than an alpine forest, although on the dryer side of the mountains, the forests quickly become more alpine.

I fished a bit where the glade came up to the lake and quickly caught a half-dozen nice-sized trout. That was it, I had all I wanted and could go home any time now. But it seemed like the day was so beautiful, and so nice and warm...and before I knew it, the night had caught up with me and I had dozed off in the sweet-smelling grasses at the edge of that little pastoral glade.

I woke with a start. Something was in the bush nearby! I could hear a heavy thump thump like something beating on a tree trunk. Now something bipedal was walking nearby in the woods, something heavy. I quickly jumped to my feet, grabbed my gear and my creel, and started back for the plane, trying hard not to run. Now something was paralleling me over in the edge of the woods.

The faster I walked, the faster the steps beside me. I looked hard, actually hoping to see a grizzly, but I knew it had to be a Sasquatch with that heavy bipedal gait. I saw nothing, and the steps stopped the minute I did. I was getting winded from being so out of shape, and I hoped it didn't start chasing me. I would never make it.

Now, as I headed back down the beach to the plane, the wood knocking started again, not far away in the thick trees. It was all I could do to not run.

My rifle had been slung over my shoulder, but I now ditched my fishing gear so I could carry the rifle in my hands, the safety unlatched. This seemed to slow down whatever was following me. It seemed to know what a gun was.

As I finally got back to where I could see the plane, I was astounded to see ravens jumping around on it and making a lot of noise. When I got closer, I could see they were all over the plane, pecking at the cloth cover.

I had never dreamed birds would destroy my beautiful Husky! Never in a million years! I had heard of ravens pecking off windshield wipers and that sort of thing on cars, but never an airplane. They found something about the cloth interesting, and had proceeded to go to pecking it full of holes, apparently making a big game out of it.

At that point, I fired the rifle into the air, and ravens scattered everywhere. I ran up to the plane, and what I saw made me want to cry. The fabric cover was full of holes, a

··· 1 2 6 ···

good 20 or 30, if not more. I was grounded, no way was that plane going anywhere.

Of all the things to happen, and especially with Sasquatch nearby.

I suddenly felt a true deep gut-wrenching fear. I was now at their mercy. Once I ran out of ammo, I was helpless, and my rifle wouldn't really do much to a creature that large anyway. And to make things worse, no one knew where I was. I had no radio contact—I was basically in a big bowl in the Coast Mountains. And I was in no shape to hike out.

I was stunned. What a strange turn of events—from being all set to take off and go home to not being able to leave at all, just in an hour or two.

I got into the plane. It felt odd with light coming in through all the holes in the fuselage. There was no way the plane was airworthy now. I just set there.

I soon noticed movement along the shoreline, maybe only a hundred feet or so away. Something was standing there, watching me. I started to panic. It was a Sasquatch, and it was making no effort to hide. But I still wasn't sure, as it was a golden color, and all the Squatch I'd heard of were brown or black. It could be a really large grizzly. It wasn't afraid of me one bit, even with the rifle. Or maybe this one hadn't seen the rifle. After all, there had been several so-called birds doing those night calls.

I felt beat. I leaned my head against the side window. It was then I noticed a little patch of duct tape I hadn't seen before where the previous owner had taped something to the inside of the window, probably some kind of paperwork.

Duct tape! I crawled into the back of the plane and opened my tool box. Duct tape, and hopefully enough to cover the holes. I pulled my fishing knife out of my pocket and set to work patching, hoping I had enough tape.

When I was done, I crawled back into the cockpit. I had patched everything pretty tight, and I was sure I could now get out. But to my horror, straight ahead of the plane, exactly where I needed to take off, stood a huge creature, at least seven feet tall. It was the Sasquatch I'd seen a bit earlier, but now that I could really make out what it was, it was terrifying. And it just stood there.

It was a beautiful creature, amazing though frightening. It was a pure golden color, and its hair was not matted, but it was very well groomed and shiny. The hair on its face was short and more of a beige color, and it had a large flat nose. It had big eyes, and the look on its face was very intent, like it meant business.

Oh man, I had to get out of there. I was no match for these guys, rifle or no, and the Husky really wasn't like other airplanes, it had only the fabric skin, not aluminum like a regular plane, not that even aluminum would've had much of a chance against these guys. But I had no protection even in the plane.

I started the engine. The rotor started turning while I pondered what to do. If the Sasquatch decided not to move, I could run it over and do it some serious damage, but it would also mean the end of my rotor. I would then be stuck there, and if he had any friends...

Now I noticed movement out the far window. I leaned forward to see two more of these creatures coming from the edge of the thick forest towards the plane. Like the first one, they were golden, and their hair was so clean it shone in the sunlight. They would take a few huge strides towards me, then would stop. Each time they stopped, they seemed to completely disappear, which I found strange and baffling. But they were definitely moving in on me, and I had to go now. I pulled the stick back a bit and the plane began to slowly move forward.

But then I stopped. I had no room here, I had to gun it and take off fast, or I would be in the water. That was the beauty of the Husky, it allowed one to land and take off in very short spaces, and that's what I had to deal with, a very short space. Behind the Sasquatch was a big log, then the lake. I couldn't try to intimidate him by moving the plane closer, I would lose my takeoff space.

The other two were now very close. A few more steps and they would be next to the plane. I thought about shooting at them, but even if my rifle would take one down, the others would be on me before I could defend myself. I still wasn't sure what they were up to—did they mean me harm or were they just curious?

That's when I noticed my fishing creel on the seat next to me. It had been clipped to my belt, and I'd taken it off when I got into the plane and forgotten all about it. Even though I'd ditched my fishing gear, I still had the creel, and in it, six nice big rainbow trout.

I opened my side window and took a big fish from the creel and tossed it as hard as I could towards the Sasquatch in front of me, but a bit towards the side. It looked at the fish, then took a few steps towards it and grabbed it. I took out two more and threw them towards the back of the plane, hoping the other two Squatch would go for them. Then I quickly threw the whole creel, remaining fish and all, towards the side of the plane where the first Squatch was now eating the fish.

As the beautiful golden Sasquatch stepped aside to grab the creel, I gunned the engine. I was in the air in seconds, a mere thirty feet of runway was all I needed, and I could see the Squatch looking at me, surprised, as I climbed literally over its head. I'll never forget that, and its big intelligent eyes stayed with me as I climbed and climbed.

As I finally got enough altitude to break out and climb back to follow the highway, I noticed my hands were shaking. It was all I could do to just concentrate on getting back out, getting to the Hill and following the road back down into the Bella Coola Valley.

When I finally got back to the airport and landed, I called Will to come and get me. There was no way I could drive myself home, and I also didn't want to be alone. Will was fascinated by my story and wanted to know exactly where the lake was, but this was before things like Google Earth existed, and it was hard to pin down. I never did fly over it again or manage to locate it on a map, even though several people I talked to wanted to go in there.

I finally got my plane repaired, to the tune of $15,000, as they had to completely redo the fabric cover. I then sold it and bought a Piper Cub, which meant I was back to the old modus operandi of having to land where there was plenty of strip. But there was no way I was ever going to risk being grounded like that again. I did miss that Husky.

I didn't give up on fishing and getting out into the wilds, but I never went alone after that. And one thing all this did for me was to make me think twice about the assumptions we all have about the world and what's out there. I can tell you one thing, we're not at the top of the food chain, that's for sure.

And I did get a new career. I started a brewery. If you're ever in the Bella Coola Valley, you'll know it by all the Sasquatch names on the brews—as well as the Lost Lake Ale, made with pure glacier water and winner of several awards. The label has an artist's rendition of that Sasquatch eating my trout.

[11] The Wild Cave

This story was told by a fellow named Jeremy who had been on several of my flyfishing trips. He loved the campfire stories and never missed one while he was with us, but he had never been involved in the telling. I always figured he didn't have a story to tell, which was OK, as we can't all have the privilege of being scared to death out in the wilds—some of us get to sit and listen while the others relate how their hearts almost stopped.

Then one evening, Jeremy decided to tell his story. It was a good one, and I've actually been into the cave he mentions, but I didn't have the good luck of meeting Uncle Hairy. (And I guess I'm grateful for my bad luck if that's what's called good luck.) —Rusty

I've only been lost twice in my life, once in a thick forest where I couldn't get my bearings, and the second time in a cave. Both times were unsettling to someone who prides themselves on being competent outdoors, and both taught me humility (which didn't last long). The worst by far was the cave (I guess it proved that I wasn't very competent indoors, either). But it wasn't being lost that got to me, it was what I found in there.

For those of you who know the Glenwood Springs, Colorado area, you'll know the surrounding Flat Tops Wilderness is riddled with caves where water has dissolved large cavities in the limestone. I used to live in Glenwood, and I've explored a few of those caves, including Hubbard Cave and Fairy Cave (now called Glenwood Caverns). I was never much of a spelunker, having a touch of claustrophobia, but I had to give it a try.

So, anyway, it was a cool overcast summer day when a friend and I decided to visit a cave just above the freeway near No Name, a residential area that lies just out of Glenwood Springs. This particular cave is known as Cave of the Clouds. It sits high in the cliffs and takes a bit of huffing and puffing to get to. The trail has since been deemed a safety hazard by the local sheriff, and people are discouraged from going up there.

It was a sunny day, and my friend Chris and I packed a lunch and drove out there, parking along the freeway. We soon headed straight up the cliffs, following the treacherous old aqueduct that hangs from them. The hike up was strenuous, but we made it, and we soon entered the cave, which has two large rooms. The first room has been heavily vandalized, but at that time still contained many stalagmites, some of the largest in Colorado.

After examining these, Chris and I went into the second room, which had a rubbly rocky surface. It was black as night in there, and our little headlamps didn't do much. We were amateur cavers and really didn't have the right equipment.

Unbeknownst to me, Chris wandered back into the first room, leaving me to my own devices. Right off, I noticed a strong stench in there, and I think that was why Chris left. I wanted to leave, but I also knew I probably wouldn't be climbing back up that cliffside anytime soon, and I wanted to check out the cave. I'd be quick, I decided.

I crawled through a couple of small squeezeways that didn't really go anywhere, then came back into the second room. Things were very black, as the dim glow in the first room didn't enter that second room. My small headlamp didn't do much, and the stench seemed to be getting worse, plus I was starting to feel kind of weird. It's hard to describe, but I just felt eerie. I decided I should just go back out and forget about exploring this one.

I stood there for bit, wondering where Chris had gone and calling out to him, but with no answer. I then jumped down from a large rock I was standing on, catching the metal water bottle attached to my belt on another smaller rock, jamming it hard into my ribs. The pain was intense, and I knew I'd probably cracked or broken a couple of ribs, having broken them once before when I got thrown from a horse. I sat down for awhile, dizzy and feeling like I might pass out from the pain.

After awhile, I decided I definitely needed to go home, so I stood up and began making my way back to what I thought was the first room. Nope, dead end, a wall. I turned around and retraced my path, hitting another wall. This went on for some time, and believe me, wandering around this room in the dark with what turned out to be two broken ribs was a challenge. I was totally disoriented at this point.

I had studied a small map on the internet that showed the layout of the cave, and I realized now I should have printed it out and brought it with me. But the cave wasn't very big, so I hadn't seen a need for a map. The only thing to watch out for was a 15-foot pit somewhere along the back wall, and I had figured that could be easily seen with a headlamp.

I sat down on a rock, not sure what to do. I was lost. I really was in no shape to be exploring, as the pain was getting more intense. I inadvertently started moaning a bit—man, there's nothing like having a broken rib. It's intense.

Let me backtrack a bit and talk about Paul McCartney—no, not the singer, but a hermit who lived near Cave of the Clouds who called himself that. He was pretty crazy, and he later ended up dying up there, in the cave he called home, not far from where I was at that moment.

Paul was in his 50s, and nobody knew his real name. He lived on some kind of small pension he got, hiking down into town once a month to cash the check and buy groceries, then hiking back up there. He was pretty territorial, and he would often run people off, even though it was federal land. Pretty much everyone who went up there knew to keep an eye out for Paul McCartney. If you get on the internet, you'll find more about him if you want—just search for "Paul McCartney Cave of the Clouds."

After what seemed like forever (but was probably about 10 minutes), I was still sitting there, now half-crying, hoping Chris would come and look for me. I was in so much pain I could barely move at that point.

I suddenly stopped, for my sixth sense told me to shut the heck up, someone or something was in there with me. I immediately thought of Paul McCartney—it was probably him. If so, he wasn't real well known for his hospitality, so I might not want to advertise my presence, though I knew it was way too late.

I sat there, real quiet, then realized the stench was getting stronger—much stronger. Man, if that was Paul McCartney, he sure needed a bath!

Now I could hear breathing, and it sounded like something really big, something with huge lungs. It was really raspy, in-out, in-out, a slow kind of deep breathing. Now I was beginning to think I was in there with a bear, and that really scared the you-know-what out of me. This is not a real large cave, mind you, and there's only one entrance, which I now couldn't find, for the life of me.

OK, imagine yourself sitting in a dark cave with broken ribs, in pain, lost, knowing you can't just stumble around trying to get out cause there's a deep pit somewhere, and your light isn't good enough to see much of where you're going. That alone is bad enough, but add a stench to the recipe, as well as something big nearby, breathing hard, and it all made me feel like I was going to throw up.

Now add a pair of red glowing eyes suddenly appearing, which aren't all that far from you. Just out of nowhere, two very large eyes, like someone plugged in a circuit or something.

That was the final straw for me. I was so scared I just got up and fled as best I could in the opposite direction. Whatever it was didn't follow me, but stayed put.

I'll have nightmares about what now happened for the rest of my life.

I turned back to see if it was following me. The eyes suddenly rose a good eight or nine feet off the ground. Whatever this thing was, it must've stood up. It then picked up a rock and lobbed it at me, barely missing me. Crap. Now what could I do? Here came another rock, then another. I ducked, but was nearly hit. The pain from moving quickly almost made me black out.

Then a small rock hit my backpack, and I just lost it, I mean lost it. I started yelling and screaming as loud as I could, hoping Chris would hear me and come help. In the meantime, this creature lobbed another rock my way.

I started inching along the wall, away from it, feeling my way and using my light as best I could. Here came another rock. I panicked and took off my headlamp, holding it out and shining it towards the creature. I had to know who or what my enemy was. I was ready to collapse, and I knew it would all be over at that point.

The light didn't show much except a big black shadowy form with glowing eyes, but it was huge, and I mean huge. I kept trying to feel my way along the wall and get away. Suddenly, I could hear Chris's voice calling out, and I started yelling again.

A light! Chris was here! I yelled out, and he came over and found me, commenting on the stench. I had no time for words, but just told him we needed to get the bleep out now, and I followed him, hanging onto the back of his belt so I wouldn't lose him.

We entered the main room, where there was more light, and he stopped, but I pushed him ahead of me in a panic, saying, "Keep going, keep going!"

We were soon out of the cave, where it had started raining. It was then that this creature started screaming like a banshee, so loud it echoed through the cavern. Chris then realized what was going on, and we both panicked and hoofed it on back down the viaduct, down the muddy cliffs, and to the car.

The worst part of the experience wasn't the broken ribs, nor the feeling of complete and total disorientation, nor the feeling of hopelessness and helplessness, but rather the sheer terror at having a Bigfoot in there with me. And I know that's what it was, especially since there have been other encounters in that area.

That was the last wild cave I've been in and will ever go into again, believe me. I still have nightmares about being in there with that wild creature. Chris says I have PTSD, and maybe so, but I do know I'll never go caving again.

[12] Lunch Guests

I have to admit to kind of liking this story, even though it scares me to think about how vulnerable we can be out in the outback. It was told around a campfire in the high country not far from where it happened, near Big Sky, Montana.

Everyone was sitting around talking over hot buttered rum, and after Brian told this, we all got real quiet. It was funny, because Montana has wolves, and just as he finished, a pack of wolves began howling in the distance, causing our hackles to stand up.

We all sat around the campfire far into the night, none of us willing to admit we were afraid to go to bed. It's nights like that, where you're half-dead from sleep deprivation, that you sometimes feel most alive. —Rusty

This story took place when I was a mere kid, only about 21 years old. Of course, at the time, I thought I was all grown up and knew everything, but this event taught me otherwise. In fact, it's been many years ago, and I still haven't really figured out the mystery of how Bigfoot can be so elusive and go unproved in the scientific world when so many have had encounters. I know I believe in the existence of this creature, and here's why.

I had recently dropped out of college at the end of my junior year. I was homesick. I came from a close family, and the only time I had really been away from them was in college. Also, I grew up in a ski town, and I missed skiing and having fun and, you know, the resort atmosphere. So, I decided to take a year off and make some money, do some skiing, then go back to school.

So, now I needed a job. Fast forward to one day when I was hanging around the ski area and someone told me the local surveyor was looking for someone. Before you can say theodolite, I was a land surveyor, a rodman, wandering around the countryside near Big Sky, Montana, trying to place an imaginary grid onto a not-so-imaginary landscape.

I initially thought I must be pretty multitalented, considering my major in school was journalism, not even vaguely related to the job. But I later realized that being a rodman was just a grunt labor job. Grab the level, go over there, OK, now go over there...you get the picture.

It was fun at first, and I did quickly advance to being the instrument person, which I initially thought was a big deal, as now I had some responsibility. But it was soon winter, and before long I realized that being the instrument person was an even worse grunt labor job than being a rodman, cause you had to carry the instrument while going here and there and everywhere.

I found myself working in the deep snows that are typical of the Montana Rockies. I worked on snowshoes or cross-country skis and usually had to dig a pit in the snow before I could set up my theodolite. Needless to say, I got to be in pretty good shape. And needless to say, most surveying companies usually take the winter off. But we had a sort of rush job to do.

We were surveying the location for a small earthen dam on a stream that flowed down through the big pines in a small steep valley. The land belonged to a local rancher who wanted to dam the waters for irrigating his hayfields in the meadows below. It really wasn't a big project, but he wanted it done ASAP so he could start construction first thing in the spring and hopefully get it operational for the summer hay crops. This is why we were stumbling around in the deep snows. Once we got done, we would take the rest of the winter off and go skiing.

My crew chief, Bob, was a serious Christian guy and prayed every time we got stuck, which was at least a twice-daily event, once going in and once coming out. My prayers were more of the type of thanking God for chains and shovels. I think Bob was kind of nervous working out there in such extreme conditions, maybe because he was responsible for everything, including our safety.

We drove an old Jeep Wagoneer that had the back window missing, which made for some chilly rides, and we typically had to build a fire to warm up after we'd finally make it in to where we were surveying, as well as build another fire to warm up at lunch time.

I think we would maybe get a good four hours of actual work in each day, considering all we had to do to get there and back and just survive. I took to carrying hot buttered rum in my thermos just to help me get through the day, though I could tell Bob didn't approve.

We decided to make a big deal of lunch each day, as we wanted it to last as long as possible. Since we already had to build a fire, we started bringing hamburgers and hot-dogs to roast, making ourselves a hot meal. I think this is what attracted our visitors, which I'll explain soon.

One day, my ski binding quit working. It was barely holding my boot onto my ski, but I managed to cope and keep working. This happened early in the day, and we should've just quit work and gone back to town and dealt with it. But since it was such an ordeal to get in and out of where we were, we tried to carry on. I did pretty well and felt like I was giving my boss a good day's work.

Lunchtime came and we stopped to build our fire and cook lunch. Today's entree was some really greasy bratwurst Bob had brought. The fat dripped into the fire and smoked and smelled up the whole woods. We didn't worry about it too much, as we knew all the bears would be hibernating, and there wasn't anything much else out there to think about. We sat there on some logs around our fire, trying to get warm while eating our brats and drinking hot cider.

It was a beautiful crisp sunny day, and I was enjoying being out in the middle of the beautiful high pines, each dusted with a coat of powder snow. Every once in awhile we'd hear a small thump as snow fell from the trees. Some-times I would feel like I was in a dream, being way out in the Colorado backcountry like that in the dead of winter, something few people got to do.

We finally put the fire out and got back to work, as much as we didn't want to. I kept working with my broken binding, but it was OK, as I didn't have to move my instrument much. That was one of the nice things about being an instrument man, the rodman had to do most of the walking. Bob would do some of it, but he generally stood by me and took down the angles I was shooting and told me where to go next.

We needed to tie into a corner section marker, and Bob and Larry, the rodman, had to go find it. It's not easy to find a section marker when it's buried under deep snow, but they were trying. They knew the general area and had shovels and were over a ways from me, digging. I was standing by my instrument, just fiddling around and waiting, hopping up and down a bit, trying to stay warm, and whistling, something I like to do cause I play the guitar and try to write songs.

I think the smell of the brats and my whistling combined to make the local Bigfoot population a bit curious, because after a bit, I stopped whistling, but the whistling kept on going for a moment. I can tell you, that got my attention, cause I knew Bob and Larry were up on the ridge quite a bit above me, digging for this marker, and no way could it be them. I could see them over beyond, and the whistling had come from over behind.

I sort of did a double take, then slowly turned in a circle, trying to spot what had made the sound. I figured it was someone out snowshoeing or maybe skiing, although it was a heck of a bad place to do either, just a steep little valley going down into a small stream. No place to ski, really.

Well, the human mind has to make sense out of the unexplained, so my mind decided it was a marmot, a whistle pig. Now, marmots hibernate in the winter, or at least they stay in their underground homes, and they really do whistle, but it's more of a sharp short loud tweet, not like a human whistling a song. But my mind said it had to be a marmot, since there wasn't any other explanation.

I relaxed and started stomping my feet in place, trying to stay warm. My girlfriend had bought me the latest in technology at the time, a pair of battery-powered socks to keep one's feet warm, and I had them on, but they weren't working. I was now in worse shape than if I'd just worn my usual wool socks. My feet were starting to feel numb.

I started singing, since I didn't want to hear any more whistling. I'm sure anyone watching me would've thought I was nuts, jumping up and down and singing in a pit in four-foot deep snow in the middle of winter. Maybe I was.

I stopped singing and stood there for a moment, assessing my situation, wondering what time it was and when I could go home, when I heard something strange.

From the same direction I'd heard the whistling, I could now hear a fluttering noise, like a very large bird flapping its wings. This was really bizarre, I'd never heard anything like it, and I had no idea what it could be. This only happened for a few seconds, then I heard something whack on a tree. Whack! It hit hard—whack, whack, whack—three times.

Now I could hear three whacks just like it, but from the distance, over towards the mountain. What the heck? I started getting nervous, and I got on my walkie-talkie to Bob.

"Bob, you guys hearing these noises?"

They answered that they were, and they had no idea what it was. I later thought that maybe the strange fluttering noise had something to do with the huge lungs these creatures, the Bigfoot, have. Maybe it was clearing its throat somehow and it made this noise. I've since read a number of encounters, but I've never read anything about this.

The sun was now getting lower, and Bob and Larry came back over. They'd decided it was time to go. They couldn't find the marker, and the whacking had kind of weirded them out. Neither had heard the whistling or fluttering noises.

The days in Montana are really short in the winter, as we're far north, and the nights are long and cold. It wasn't prudent to cut it too close—it was best to get an early start back, so we loaded everything up and started the ski trip back to the Wagoneer.

I was in the rear, and something made me look back, some hunch, maybe. I couldn't see very well through the trees, but it looked like there were two large black figures over where Bob and Larry had been digging, and they also looked like they were digging. Maybe they were trying to figure out what Larry and Bob were after.

This gave me the cold chills, and I was already cold enough. I yelled at the guys to wait up, and they did. They were down the trail a bit, around a small curve. I caught up and told them what I had seen.

"Let's get the hell out of here, now!" Bob said. Larry and I were both surprised to hear him cuss, as he was usually so serious and pretty religious.

"Keep your walkie-talkies on. Try not to get too far ahead of me—I'm still having trouble with this binding," I told them.

Bob stopped and got some string out of his pack, and we sat down in the snow. Using the string, he wrapped the binding onto the ski, holding it tight. It felt good now, and I wasn't so nervous about keeping up. The sun was now low in the sky, and the trees had long shadows. We needed to get back. We were about a half-mile from the vehicle, all fairly steep downhill.

I was again keeping up the rear, as ice was now collecting around the string, building up into a sort of brake until it would fall off and I could move freely again. This cycle repeated itself as I tried to ski along. I constantly had to hop along trying to keep the ski under my foot, as the ice would cause the ski to turn. I had three-pin toe bindings with no heel support.

All this slowed me down considerably. The snow was too deep to walk out. My colleagues left me in the dust, so to speak, and it was soon nearly dark. I tried to call them on the walkie-talkie, but all I got was static.

Oh sweet holy Scooby Doo, what I saw then would have really set Bob to praying. Larry, too—in fact, I wanted to pray, but I was too scared.

Two sets of huge tracks veered out of the forest and directly onto the path ahead of me. Whatever made them was huge, and they sank clear down into the trail, even though we'd packed it pretty good coming in. These things were ahead of me, but behind Bob and Larry. They appeared to be following the guys. I wondered if they knew I was back here.

Their big deep tracks made the going even harder for me, as they pitted the trail. I didn't want to come upon these things anyway, so I decided to get off trail and try to navigate my way back by what few cues I could—the sun and my own sense of direction. I stepped off the trail, went about 50 feet to my left, then angled back, trying to parallel where I thought the trail was going. I knew that I wasn't very likely to get lost, as the trail followed the creek back down the valley, for the most part.

Now I was extremely anxious, wondering if I would get back alright. But I carried onward, having no choice, really cold and a bit bitter that the rest of my crew had just left me like that. I decided to cross the creek for added safety. No way did I want to run into those two big things, whatever they were.

I managed to get across the little creek on some slippery rocks, which was a miracle, considering I was on skis and carrying a heavy instrument over my shoulder.

The shadows were lengthening, and the temperature was dropping fast. Now I could hear voices yelling in the distance. I hoped it wasn't the devious Windigo of Canadian fame, luring me to my demise. Or the two Bigfoot, if that's what they were. The noise came from down the valley about where I thought the Wagoneer was. I got back on the radio again, but nobody answered.

Now I was down the valley far enough that I knew I had to be close to the road and the Wagoneer. I decided to cross back over the stream and find the trail again. It wasn't long before I intersected it, and now the huge tracks were going back up the trail, back uphill. I shivered. Were they looking for me? Would they come back?

If I could've taken off those damn skis and run, that would've been good. That's what I wanted to do, but the snow was just too deep. So I kept plodding along, down the trail to the Wagoneer.

I was soon standing beside the vehicle, and there was no one there. Now I was really panicked. How could I have beat them here? Had they turned back to look for me and we passed each other? Maybe getting off trail wasn't such a good idea. Yet I knew if I hadn't, the creatures would've run smack into me.

We never locked our vehicle, mostly because there was no point in it, with the back window broken out, plus we were always way out in the boonies. I placed the instrument into the back, then took off my skis, glad to be rid of them. I once again tried the radio, but with no luck. Now I was truly worried.

I sat and waited in the car, but nobody came. It was now almost dark, the sun long ago having gone down over the valley rim. I had no idea what to do. Bob had the car keys. I got out and looked around the car, trying to see if they'd come back, but it was impossible to tell if the boot tracks were from this morning or later this afternoon.

I hiked a bit back up the trail, post-holing into the snow, looking to see if I could make sense of the ski tracks, but everything was all jumbled. At least there were no Bigfoot tracks, they hadn't come down to the vehicle. And Larry hadn't left his rod here, which would make sense if they'd come back and then gone looking for me. I was beginning to think they had never showed up.

I had to act quickly. No way could I go back up the trail and look for them, even if I wanted to—my binding was shot. And no way could I sit there in the cold all night. I decided to walk out to the nearest paved road, about three miles away.

I pulled my little surveyor's notebook out of my jacket pocket and left a note on the dash, telling them what I'd done. I was beginning to think they needed help. It was kind of ironic, since I'd been the one who needed help earlier with my bad binding.

The road out wasn't too bad, as our Wagoneer had packed it down pretty well, and I made good time, walking where the snow was crusted. I was maybe a good mile out when I heard a chilling sound—it was like a deep roar and bellowing combined, and it shook the air waves with its power. It sounded like it was several miles away, but I still took off running, scared more than I've ever been before or since.

Before too long, I was at the main road and had flagged someone down. There was no cell phone reception, so we had to drive the fifteen miles back into town before we could call the sheriff. The person who gave me a ride was kind enough to take me home, and the first thing I did was put my cold feet by the fireplace.

I had explained everything to the dispatcher, and they said they would contact me soon. They were going to launch a search and rescue team. They might need my help, so I was to stay put. I managed to eat a little dinner and get warmed up. Then I waited.

I finally got a call, about three hours later, when I was feeling desperately concerned about Bob and Larry. The search and rescue team had found them, and they were nowhere near the vehicle. They had become disoriented and were sitting by a fire about a half-mile off-trail. They had heard the rescuers calling and started yelling back.

Their story was really strange. They had been skiing back to the vehicle, thinking I was close behind. They'd actually stopped several times to call out for me, and they thought I had answered. Something had answered, anyway, and they thought it was me, though they couldn't make out what I was saying. They continued on, thinking I was right behind them.

But things started to get stranger and stranger. They were only about a tenth of a mile from the vehicle when they could hear me calling out, as if I needed help. They turned around and came back up the trail.

They called to me, and I would call back, but they couldn't seem to get any closer, no matter how far they walked up the trail, I was always just beyond sight. By now, it was getting close to dusk. Just then, Bob spotted the same type of tracks I'd seen earlier. He put two and two together, remembering the odd noises earlier.

He and Larry were totally terrified. They feared the worst for me, and they now realized they were being lured by something. They didn't know what to do—keep going back up the trail and look for me, or go back to the Wagoneer?

But then they froze in their tracks where they were, as they now heard a whooping noise coming from the trail right ahead of them. This was followed by the same type of call immediately behind them. They were surrounded!

They stood there, then took off without saying a word into the trees. It was nearly dark, and they had no idea where they were going, only that they had an irresistible urge to flee.

They skied along as best they could, catching their ski tips in the undergrowth, nearly crashing and burning many times, until they finally came to a small clearing. It was then they heard the same chilling sound I had heard down below, the deep roar and bellowing combined, and it was very close—so close they could feel the air vibrate.

They decided to stay put, and quickly began gathering wood for a fire. By the time it was dark, they had managed to build a small fire near a big Douglas fir tree, where the snow wasn't as deep. It was here they huddled together, near the fire, scared to death. They could again hear the whooping noises, and soon the dark figures were nearby. Larry said they could barely make them out, standing a ways back in the shrubs, at the edge of the clearing.

The whooping continued, then dissolved into a round of wood knocking, then went back to the whooping. Larry was worried they were calling in reinforcements.

Finally, Bob could take no more, and he took off his day pack, which still held bratwurst and bread and some cheese. He took out the food and threw it as far as he could, into the circle of darkness outside the fire.

Before long, they saw a huge figure step from the shadows, quickly grabbing the food and retreating. By then, it was so dark they could only make out its shape and size, and it was huge. Bob told Larry it had to be a Bigfoot.

Now the creatures seemed to retreat, and the guys heard no more night noises, but they were too scared to leave the fire, plus they had no idea where they were relative to the trail. They would have to stay and wait out the long bitterly cold night and hope they could find enough wood to survive. Bob started praying in earnest.

It wasn't too very long before they could hear yelling, and they knew it was someone out looking for them. They took their chances and started yelling back. It was the rescuers.

This incident made me decide to end my surveying career. I quit the next day.

Last I heard, Larry had moved to Florida, and Bob had gone on to become a preacher back in Kansas. Maybe thinking about the fires of hell was preferable to standing around the fires in the backcountry shivering, waiting for Bigfoot. I don't know, but I suspect it would be.

[13] Peddling with Disaster

· ·

This story was told by a woman around a campfire on one of my guided trips near Quake Lake in Wyoming. It's the rare tale of someone who was possibly harmed by a Bigfoot, though nobody really knows for sure what happened. I myself am voting for some other explanation, as we all know the Big Guy is typically harmless (as long as you heed the calls to leave his territory, which most of us do).

But, like all animals, it's very possible there are rogue Bigfoot who seem to be having a bad hair day. In any case, this story tells us we should always be careful and never underestimate our fragility as mere humans on a big wild planet. —Rusty

My name is Josie and I'm telling my story for the first time. I mean, I've talked to a couple of close friends about it, and they've told me that sharing it might lessen the trauma— maybe telling it here will help me come to grips with it.

I used to love to mountain bike. It was my escape from my stressful job as a computer programmer. And I love nature, so mountain biking got me outside and away from all the trappings of civilization.

One day I was over in Crested Butte, Colorado, a mountain biking mecca, doing a wildflower ride with my friend and co-worker Amy. It was summer, and the flowers were just everywhere—columbine, mountain daisies, all kinds of stuff. We were having a great time.

We stopped to take a break and have lunch when up came a lone rider. It was a guy, and he was kind of geeky looking, tall and skinny and pale and looked like he'd never been outside more than an hour in his life.

He stopped and talked for a bit, and we invited him to hang out and have lunch with us, as he hadn't brought anything and looked pretty pitiful.

Anyway, this guy's name was Dave, and he also worked in the computer industry. I was a programmer in Boulder, Colorado, and Dave worked over in nearby Broomfield at another company. My company did 3-D modeling for aircraft simulators, and Dave's did something with database software. We were all cubicle slaves, even though we made good money.

We sat there, the three of us, talking about everything under the sun, and finally it was time to head back, so we rode back to town. We ended up having dinner together, and this was the start of the whole fiasco.

Seems Dave, like so many of us cubicle slaves, wanted to start his own business. This was almost an epidemic in the industry, as the burnout rate was so high. I worked with one couple who actually quit extremely lucrative jobs to go run a Dairy Queen in some little town in Kansas, and they loved it.

Dave told us that he was going to start a mountain-bike company—take people out on tours. We talked about the mechanics of that for a bit, and I had some ideas, you know, places to go and how to advertise, stuff like that. He wanted my email address, so I gave it to him, not really expecting to hear from him again.

We ended the evening wishing him well, and Amy and I went and sat in the hot tub at our hotel and promptly forgot all about it. You know how people talk and few do anything. We figured Dave was just talking.

The summer continued on, and I was out biking literally every weekend. Soon it was fall, and I took off and spent a couple of weeks over in the canyon country, mountain biking. I forgot all about Dave.

It was the next spring, in April, and there on my computer was an email from Dave. He had started his company and needed someone to help out as backup. He had bought a support vehicle, hired a guide, advertised in the bike magazines, and now had several tours booked. He would be the support vehicle driver, but he would feel better if he had a couple of people along who would be there on his first tour just in case. Would Amy and I be interested in coming along? We wouldn't make anything, but we would get our expenses paid.

I asked for specifics. Dave said the tour would take three days, and we would be riding across two four-wheel-drive passes in Colorado's San Juan Mountains. We'd stay in B&Bs and have full vehicle support in case someone got tired or sick.

The trip was kind of a yuppie affair in that all one had to do was ride all day and then lounge around sipping wine in a hot tub in the evening at a B&B after dinner. Of course, the rides would be tough, so the luxuries would be well earned.

I called Amy. It didn't take long to come to a consensus.

We were excited. A three-day tour, staying in nice B&Bs in Colorado resort towns, and all for free. Who in their right mind would say no?

The tour was booked for late June, as that was about the earliest time that one could be sure the mountain passes would be open. It was soon time, and Amy and I drove to where the tour would begin.

The route started in Lake City, went over Cinnamon Pass into Silverton, then over Ophir Pass, spending the night in the small town of Ophir, then an easy cruise into Telluride for the last day. If you've ever been over any of these passes, you know what high-altitude riding means—10,000 plus feet.

The first day went well, as it wasn't a long ride, just up and over the pass and down into the scenic town of Silverton. It started raining during the afternoon and we all arrived muddy, wet, and tired, but that made the gourmet dinner that much better. After dinner, everyone went to the restaurant bar, where we had a great time talking. The group had about twelve people.

The next day, we left Silverton for Ophir. We spread out, each riding the pace they liked, and eventually made our way up to the top of Ophir Pass. Keep in mind that none of these passes see anything but four-wheel-drive traffic, as they're not paved and are rocky and steep. So we saw hardly anyone besides our group.

Amy had hit it off with a guy from Lake Tahoe and was riding with him, which left me to cruise on down the pass alone. I stopped and took lots of photos, especially of the wildflowers, which were really nice. The group was mostly ahead of me, with the support vehicle bringing up the rear, providing water and snacks.

Ophir Pass quickly drops down into the tiny town of Ophir, once a gold and silver mining hub, but now a bedroom community for the ski town of Telluride. The road was all downhill and wouldn't take us long to get there, so I decided to stop and take a break. I pulled my bike off the road and hid it in some bushes, then headed for a small rock outcropping above the road. It looked like it would make a great place to get some panoramic shots.

I climbed out onto the rocks, my feet dangling over the edge, and took lots of photos of the valley and of the riders as they cruised down the switchbacks below me.

Amy and her new friend cruised by, talking and laughing, and soon the support vehicle had also passed me. I knew I should go, as I didn't want them worrying about me, and they would do a tally once they all got to the B&B in Ophir.

I was putting my camera away when I noticed someone coming down the road, staying a bit back from the support vehicle. It was really odd, because this person was dressed in black from head to toe. They appeared to be on foot. As they came closer, something told me to get out of view, so I slipped down into the rocks and watched as they passed below me.

Pardon the bluntness, but I nearly peed my pants. What I saw was no human, but a large creature that looked like a football player on steroids and then some. It was kind of loping along, its very long arms dangling clear down below the knees. It acted like it was following the bikers, as it seemed to purposely hold back just enough to not be seen.

It had a conical head, with the neck kind of melting down into huge shoulders. It also seemed to be very aware of the road behind it, like it didn't want anyone coming up unseen from the rear, as it would look behind it a lot.

I had no idea what to do. Then it dawned on me, take a picture—no one is going to believe you, take a picture! I pulled my camera back out of my daypack and managed to snap a couple of shots before it loped on down the road. I was still using an old film camera I had, and I later wished I had brought my little digital camera, because then I could have shown the photos to everyone as proof. But my film camera took better wildflower photos, as I had an expensive macro lens for it.

I continued to just sit there, then I started shaking uncontrollably. I couldn't stop. Then I started crying from fear. What if it came back and saw me? How would I ever catch up with everyone, with that thing between me and them? My legs felt like rubber, and I just sat there in the rocks. In fact, I had squeezed myself so far down into the rocks that I wasn't sure I could get back out.

Then I heard the sound of vehicles coming down the road. I quickly came to my senses, pulled myself from the rocks and ran down to the road, arriving just as a couple of Jeeps came around the corner. I flagged them down.

They stopped, and I told them I was sick. Could I hitch a ride with them to Ophir? They were very kind and managed to bungee cord my bike to the rear of one of the Jeeps, and off we went. I worried that we would come upon the black creature, but it must have heard us and stepped off the road into the bushes, as we didn't see anything.

That night I stayed in my room. I wasn't in the mood to socialize, and I couldn't eat. Amy didn't notice, as she was distracted by her budding romance. I worried about what I had seen and wondered if I should tell the group so they could be on alert. I knew they would think I was crazy, but I also didn't want anyone's safety to be compromised.

I couldn't sleep all night, tossing and turning. Finally, at dawn, I got up and went outside for a bit. The small community was still asleep, and the sun hadn't yet crested over the high mountains cradling the town. I sat there for a bit on the porch of the B&B, watching the world slowly awaken, and that's when I heard the strangest and most unsettling sound I've ever heard.

It sounded like a siren coming from high in the forest above town, a place where there were no roads, as it was too rugged and steep. How could there be a siren up there? It carried for a long ways, and it had an organic sound to it, like it wasn't mechanically generated—and it went on and on and on. Whatever was making it had huge lungs! This went on for a few minutes, then it turned into a long drawn-out kind of yodeling sound, made by something with a very deep bass voice.

I was chilled to my core. I had to tell everyone. They needed to know this thing had been following them. But from the sounds of it, it had gone back up into the mountains. I didn't know what to do. I didn't want everyone to think I was a lunatic, but I felt a strong need to warn them.

The B&B host came out with a cup of coffee for me, and I asked him to sit down for a moment. I told him what I had just heard. His face turned white as a sheet.

He at first tried to say it was nothing, but I told him I knew what it was as I had seen it. He gave me a long look, like he was trying to figure out if I were trustworthy, then told me that this thing had started coming around the area last summer, and everyone was terrified of it. But they were equally terrified that word would get out and they would lose the little business they had.

I kind of laughed and told him I thought something like that would probably increase business. Just then, Amy came out and the B&B owner excused himself to go start breakfast. I decided to tell Amy and see what she thought.

After I told her, Amy sat there for a bit, not saying a word. She then told me she had thought she'd seen something several times from the corner of her eye yesterday, but then when she would look, there was nothing there. She looked scared. I told her I had taken photos of the thing.

We went in for breakfast, and both Amy and I said almost nothing. I was still trying to decide whether or not to tell everyone. I finally decided I had to, but I would wait until we were getting on the road again.

I had decided to ride in the support vehicle. I'd lost my taste for biking. I just wanted to be home, safe and sound in my little house. I tried to talk Amy into riding in the support vehicle with me, but she wanted to ride with her new boyfriend.

After breakfast, I pulled Dave aside and told him what I'd seen. His reaction didn't surprise me one bit. He looked at me like I was crazy. When I told him I was concerned for the group, he basically told me I was worried about nothing and that I had probably hallucinated something.

He made me feel like I was nuts, and I knew he was worried about his tour money. He didn't want people freaking out and going home, as he was afraid they would want a refund. I pretty much lost any respect I had for him, though I did try to see it his way—but I couldn't.

But then I wondered if maybe I wasn't being overly protective, and since this last leg of the tour was short and not really in the backcountry, I decided I would just keep my mouth shut. Amy and Dave both knew what I'd seen, so they could spread the word if they wanted.

The group all took off, riding on down to the highway, then along it for a bit, then taking off onto a side road that went down by the old powerplant at Ames, famous for being the first AC current plant, built by Tesla. The group would then eventually loop back onto the highway and ride into Telluride. I figured the odds of the creature following along were pretty slim, as this part of the ride wasn't remote at all.

I was apparently wrong.

I rode along in the support vehicle with Dave, making no bones about why. No way was I going to ride with that beast out there. I was still in shock from my encounter with it, even though it hadn't even seen me. Dave continued to treat me like I was crazy—until we caught up with Amy's new friend, that is.

He was standing with his bike by the side of the road, waving us down. Amy had stopped and gone into the bushes to pee, but she hadn't come back out. He had waited a bit, then started calling for her, with no response. He'd then gone a bit back into the bushes to look, but she was totally gone. She had told him earlier about what I'd seen, and he was really panicked.

We stopped and got out and started looking in the bushes for her, sticking together, calling and yelling, but with no reply. I was now worried sick.

As soon as Dave realized Amy was truly missing, he went ballistic. He dialed 911 with his cell phone and got the sheriff's office. Two deputies were soon there, as we weren't that far from Telluride. They began their own search. Since Amy hadn't been missing all that long, they weren't as worried as I was. They figured she had just become disoriented and would soon be found.

But she wasn't. It was now getting on late afternoon, and no Amy. Dave had gone ahead into town to catch up with everyone else at the B&B and explain what was going on. Amy's new friend and I stayed with the deputies.

As soon as Dave left, I told the deputies about my encounter. I didn't care if they thought I was crazy. They now looked even more concerned. They told me that I wasn't the only one who had reported seeing this thing. Now they called out search and rescue, although normally they would have waited longer to be sure she hadn't taken off on her own or something.

The once-quiet afternoon became a beehive of activity, with SAR people arriving and heading out in various directions. I felt a sense of futility, as I somehow knew she was gone. We'd ridden many trails together, and I knew Amy could take care of herself. She would never get lost like this, right by the road, she was too savvy.

To make a long story short, they never found Amy, even after days of searching. They brought in search dogs, and the dogs refused to go out. They started shaking when they brought them to the area where Amy had disappeared.

Everyone noticed a strong garbage smell, and they found a place where the bushes had been broken and beaten down, like something big had been there. And one searcher found a series of very large tracks in the mud by a little nearby stream.

The rest of the biking group went on home the next day, as the tour was over, but I stayed on in Telluride, hoping for some news about Amy.

Nothing. I was too afraid to go searching on my own, and the sheriff had told me not to, that they didn't need two missing persons.

I finally had to leave and go back to work. I was heartsick. Amy had been a friend for a long time, and I somehow felt responsible. I shouldn't have let her ride that day. But if not, maybe the Bigfoot would have taken someone else, if that's what had happened.

But I also had virtually no evidence that the creature had harmed Amy. Most Bigfoot are supposedly harmless. There have been many encounters where no one was injured, even though the creature could easily have killed them. In fact, there have been a few accounts where Bigfoot helped people.

Maybe Amy just got lost. The forests there are thick, and there are bears, although it's rare they would harm someone. But maybe she became disoriented and had a run-in with a mama bear. But it was very rare for someone to just disappear. But I knew Amy, and she was too smart to get lost right next to the road. And she would have eventually found her way back.

The mystery has never been solved, even to this day. I'll never know what happened and whether or not it had anything to do with the creature whose photos I have in my desk drawer. They're pretty fuzzy, as I had such a short time to take them and the Bigfoot was moving so quickly, but you can tell this is something different.

I'll always wonder if Amy also saw what I saw that terrifying day.

[14] Black Hand at Box Canyon

• •

Here's another chilling story, this one told by a gal named Julie who was on a guided trip with her husband on Colorado's Yampa River. This story illustrates a side of Bigfoot I hope I never meet. —Rusty

If you're familiar with the annual Ouray Ice Festival in Colorado, you'll know the setting for my story. My name is Julie, and I grew up just a few miles down the road from Ouray. It's a beautiful town, a popular tourist destination, as it's surrounded by high peaks and also beautiful red rocks. They call it the Switzerland of America.

Box Canyon, where the ice festival is held, is an impressive deep narrow gorge that spills from the high San Juan Mountains that surround Ouray. The area is popular for ice climbing in the winter, but in the summer, after the snow and ice are gone, visitors can view the gorge from an enclosed catwalk that takes you right under Box Canyon Falls. In the spring, the thundering water is scary.

I had an up-close and personal look at the gorge one time, even though it's hard to see such things in the dark. The Ice Festival always reminds me of my good fortune at still being alive, for I think luck was all that saved me that dark and stormy night, as Snoopy would say.

It was a very high water year in Colorado—there was unusually deep snowfall, and all the rivers were raging. It was spring, and me and two friends decided it would be really epic to go visit the thundering falls in the light of the full moon.

Of course, this is slightly illegal, since the falls are one of those wonderful places that have been appropriated by clever capitalists who want to make a fast buck off things that truly should belong to us all. In other words, the area is fenced and one has to pay a fee to visit.

We wanted to see it in the full moon, and the darn place was closed at night, so how else to see it but crawl over the fence? This is a skill we learned well when we were kids and didn't have the money to get into events at the local fairgrounds.

All went well, as we made it over the 6-foot fence and on down onto the catwalk above the falls, which was a once-in-a-lifetime thing to see, record flows, just beautiful and very primal and scary in the moonlight. We stood there and hooted and hollered for some time—then, not willing to leave well enough alone, we decided to go up above the falls, where there's another lookout.

It was pretty bright out with the full moon, plus we had flashlights. We took off, hiking the trail that winds up the hill above the canyon. Once up there, we hung around awhile, again hooting and making all kinds of noise in our excitement.

We finally headed back down the trail. As usual, I was the last one, holding up the rear, just walking along, when all of a sudden I could feel the hair stand up on the back of my neck. I was being followed!

I've since done a lot of research on this, and I recall reading one account on the internet where some campers near Ouray reported hearing all sorts of strange calls during the night. The San Juan Mountains are a hotbed of activity, with quite a few accounts.

What am I talking about? Bigfoot. Right here, in the heart of some of Colorado's most incredible mountains.

Anyway, as I was walking along, keeping up the rear, I felt totally spooked all of a sudden. I stopped and listened. It was faint, but I swore I could hear a swish swish noise behind me a ways. The swish swish noise was caused by the thick bushes lining the narrow trail, and whatever it was, it was big enough that it was hitting the bushes as it walked along, making them swish.

Now I could no longer see the flashlights ahead of me. My friends were gone. I panicked. I needed to catch up. What was I thinking to stop? I started running as fast as one dares down a narrow path next to a deep gorge.

I wanted to cry out, but now I was too terrified. I didn't want whatever it was to know I was alone, nor that I was a woman. Crying out would also convey the terror I felt, and I knew it was better to not let on when you're scared of something. I learned that in the context of a friend who had once been stalked by a cougar.

She was hiking a trail over by Boulder, Colorado, and when she realized a cougar was following her, she started running in a panic, which is the worst possible thing to do. Fortunately for her, she quickly came upon some other hikers who scared the animal away.

But I knew this was no cougar. It was making way too much noise, and it had to be big to be hitting the bushes on either side of the trail. I'm not very religious, but I started praying, I was so scared. And now it was getting closer, and I could hear a thump thump as it moved along the trail, the sound of something very large and heavy coming down on the ground, something with two feet!

The San Juans have plenty of bears, but they are generally shy and leave people alone, unless you leave food around. But they don't walk on two legs. Was this possibly a person, another human? Some madman out hiking in the moonlight? Not very likely. It was just too big. And it had no light, so it had to have good night vision.

I was still running, but the trail was now going a little uphill, and I was getting tired. Whatever was following me was not running, it had a huge stride and was easily keeping up with me. In fact, it was gaining, and I could now hear it breathing. I guessed it was maybe a mere 20 feet behind me.

I was now getting winded. I was in good shape, but I've never been much of a runner. I get out of breathe too easily. I can hike at a steady pace till the cows come home, even uphill, but when I start running, I get winded fast. A friend once told me I needed to learn how to breathe properly, but I never have. But at the altitude I was at, it wasn't all that easy to breathe anyway.

I started getting stomach cramps. My lungs were burning, and I could barely keep on. And yet whatever was behind me was steady, its breathing was regular, like it was making no effort at all. I could hear it above my own puffing, so I knew it was close. And very large.

I was mystified—why, with all this running, hadn't I yet come upon my friends? How could they be that far ahead of me? And I saw no lights, nothing. It was like they had mysteriously disappeared.

I wanted to stop. I could go no further, but yet I couldn't stop. I had to keep fleeing.

Finally, I had such a bad catch in my side, the pain was so tremendous, that I just keeled over, right there on the trail. I dropped to my knees, and my flashlight tumbled from my hand. I hurt so bad I didn't care if I died, I was going to die anyway from lack of oxygen.

I kept on going down, I couldn't even stay on my knees. I rolled a bit to my side, and the next thing I knew, I was off the trail, falling into thin air. It was a feeling I don't care to repeat, but I will say it certainly makes one feel alive, wondering if this is how you're going to die.

It all happened so fast that it's hard to recall exactly what did happen, but next thing I knew, I was crammed between a large bush and the cliff, feet dangling into the abyss, just like in the movies. I was still totally silent, I was still aware enough to keep my wits about me and not start yelling, though I wanted to, believe me.

It finally dawned on me what had happened, and I then tried really hard to control my breathing so as not to gasp and make noise. Maybe the thing following me hadn't noticed my fall and had kept on going. It was difficult, but I was able to be pretty quiet, considering.

I could feel the bush start to bend a bit, and I knew it was all that kept me from falling into the deep gorge, over one-hundred feet to the rocky bottom and the raging creek. Even if I survived the fall, I would drown in the dangerous waters.

I managed to grab the bush and hold on and gradually caught my breath. I just hung there for dear life, literally, in the bright moonlight, crammed between that bush and the rocky cliff. I finally managed to look up, trying to see how far the top was above me, and it was then that I saw it, standing there, looking down at me, its glowing eyes maybe ten feet above.

I must have gone into shock, because all I can remember is a pair of green eyes staring down at me from a massive black body. The eyes were steady and didn't blink and were very hypnotic. I remember feeling very sleepy, but I knew if I went to sleep I would probably fall, so I quit looking at it.

It was then that it started making the strangest noise I've ever heard. It was a combination of a clicking and a low rumbling noise, like a faraway train. I don't remember anything that happened after that. It was as if I went to sleep or had my memory erased. But I didn't fall from the bush, so I must have been awake, but I just don't recall anything.

I don't know what happened, but that clicking noise seemed to go right through my brain, and it left me with a headache that lasted three days, and I vaguely remember this big black hand grabbing my shirt, trying to get hold of me.

Finally, I could hear voices in the distance. It was as if I'd been asleep or something—it felt like a gap of time was missing. I looked back up, and the creature was gone. I started yelling at the top of my lungs.

Before long, my friends came running, shining their lights off the edge until they spotted me. The canyon wall had a bit of an inward tilt where I was at, and they managed to somehow drag me back up onto the trail, whereupon I just lay there in shock, trying to process what had just happened. I couldn't even talk.

I finally was able to get up, and we slowly made our way back to the car, me in the middle as we walked down the trail. If that lowly bush hadn't been there, I know I wouldn't be telling story right now.

Later, after a few days when I had regained enough stability to talk about it, we discussed what had happened that night. I apparently took off on a side trail when I started running, thus not catching up with my friends. They had quickly realized I wasn't with them and had backtracked all the way to the top, fearing the worst, but had missed me, since I was on the side trail.

As they stood there at the top in the moonlight, trying to decide what to do, they also heard the sound I described. They said it had both a terrifying and calming effect on them. They knew I was where it was coming from and needed help, so they started walking towards it, but the sound soon stopped.

They searched for me for a good ten minutes before they finally heard me yelling and found me. They never saw anything, but they believed my story about the black creature when I told them what had happened.

So now, when I see the ice climbers at Box Canyon, I think back to that night and feel that I already know what it feels like to fall, though fortunately, not to land.

I thought about going back up there and throwing a bottle of wine off the edge to thank the canyon gods for my good fortune, but, thinking back to that night, I decided to just drink it instead. No way I'll ever go up there again.

[15] Do the Monster Twist

• •

I think this is one of the scariest stories I've ever heard around a campfire. It was told on a dark night high in the Sierras, where I was camping with a bunch of flyfishing addicts. Bigfoot are scary enough, but add in a tornado and you're in for a ride. —Rusty

My name is Joe, and when this story happened, I lived on a small farm in southeastern Nebraska. It was a number of years ago, and I've since left tornado country and now live in Idaho. I can tell you, I don't miss that place one bit.

My wife, Sandy, and I lived out in the country in a farmhouse, about a mile from a small agricultural town. I was working at the local hardware store, and she worked for a motel in the evenings as a night-desk person. We had both landed in this small town as the result of my aunt being ill with nobody else to take care of her, so we left our place in Wyoming and went to help her out.

The farm belonged to my aunt, Marie, although at that time she no longer lived there, having had to move into an apartment in town because of her health. My uncle, Lynn, had died several years back.

My wife would spend the day with Marie, taking care of her, then one of the neighbors would keep an eye out during the night. That way, we had everything covered. This went on for some time, then my aunt finally passed away, and my brother and I inherited the farm. Sandy and I had originally planned on staying there, but when we realized what we were getting into, we decided to leave and sold it.

It was a pretty place, as farms in Nebraska go. It was in the rolling hills, and what hadn't been turned into agricultural land still had a bit of tallgrass prairie and some thick woods that curved and followed a small stream.

There was plenty of wildlife, deer and pheasants and such, and it had a very peaceful feeling to it. I had lots of fond memories there, as my parents would always let my brother and I stay there during part of our summer vacation.

A big old barn was part of the farm's charm, and though it was by then tipping and looking a bit unsteady, it had overseen many a happy day of adventures and escapades. My brother and I had many great times on the farm, exploring the thickets and groves and wandering all over the place.

So, I was happy to go back and help my aunt, although I was sad she was in such bad shape. She had leased the land out to a corn farmer, so she had some income from that, and that freed her (and us) from worrying about taking care of everything.

We arrived in late September, kind of towards the tail end of tornado season, so that was one less thing to worry about. Nebraska is in Tornado Alley, and it's had its share of big destructive storms. We did hear the sirens in town go off once, but nothing happened.

We moved our stuff into the house, though we didn't really need much, as my aunt had left all her furniture and everything—stuff from her parents, my grandparents, who had been the original farmers there.

This included a whole house full of antique furniture, most of it very nice, and we took it all when we left, giving it to our kids and my brother to divide up. Sandy and I didn't want any of it, as we moved into a condo after leaving the farm, as we wanted to travel. But I'm getting off-track from the story here.

We were soon able to find work, as I mentioned, and since we weren't paying rent, we did OK. Our main objective was to care for Marie, not make money, but we did need to make enough to live on. Sandy's job was just four hours a day, from six to ten p.m.—she wanted to make some money to send one of our daughters who was having a rough time, and my job made what we needed to live on. But the arrangement didn't leave us much time together, as she'd be coming home about when I was going to bed.

Well, we'd been there about a month when one night, Sandy came in late and was a bit spooked. She'd seen something really big hanging out near the barn, and it looked like a bear or something. Her headlights had caught it for just a second, long enough for her to know something was amiss, but then it had stepped around the edge of the barn and was gone. There was no way she was going to go out there to see what it could be, she was too scared.

I went out on the porch with my spotlight and shined it all around, but I didn't see a thing. I told her it was probably nothing, and the shadows had been playing tricks on her eyes. I did note that the nights were getting cold and the growing season was over, and maybe whatever it was had been attracted by the field corn now drying on the stalks in the field. The farmer would soon be along to harvest.

Sandy was a bit put out that I didn't really believe her, but yet she had to agree that it was unlikely anything upright like a bear would be there. This was aggie land, and most of the wildlife of any size had been pushed out long ago, along with the Pawnee Indians.

Life went on and we both forgot about whatever it was she saw. The field corn was harvested. Part was sold, and part stored in several small silos on the farm, and the farmer then leased the fields to a cattleman who ran his herd in there for a couple of weeks until the remnant corn and stalks had been eaten, then moved them onto someone else's fields. Now the farm was quiet, with nothing going on.

It was now deep winter, December, and cold. Nebraska winters are famous (or I should say infamous), and this area was no exception. It seemed like an especially hard winter was coming on, lots of wind and snow and really cold temperatures.

The snows had really come this year, or so the locals said. The farm had about two feet in the fields, and the drifts were even higher. I had managed to hire a neighbor to plow our long drive, or we would've been walking up to the highway. And it was so cold—I would go out in the crisp cold mornings to start the cars and there would be ice crystals hanging in the air, making it hard to breathe.

One morning, as I was scraping ice off the windshield, I noticed what looked like tracks going over to the barn from the field. I walked over to investigate, curious what was coming around that would make tracks that big.

It was hard to really make out what they were, since the snow was so powdery and light that it kind of sifted into the tracks, but I did note they were big. I thought again of what Sandy had seen, even though that had been some time ago.

I wanted to pace off the stride, but the snow was too deep, but I guessed it to be a good three or four feet. Whatever had made the tracks was large. And it really liked like it walked on two feet, not four, as there was no overstride like a four-legged animal would have, where the back feet step into the prints of the front.

I went back into the house, where Sandy was getting ready to go to Marie's, and told her what I'd seen. I really didn't want to worry her, but I did want her to know something was out there.

She wasn't real thrilled to hear the news, I can assure you, and we both decided it would be prudent to be careful, especially after dark. I did note that I hadn't seen any tracks coming back from the barn area, so maybe the animal had kept on going around back and left. The barn door was latched, so I also didn't worry about something going inside. All that was in there anyway was some of the sharecropper's equipment.

We both left for the day, and when I came home that evening it was dark, as the days were short, so I didn't notice anything amiss. Same with Sandy when she got home around 10:30. All was quiet.

But the next morning, when out again warming up the cars, I noticed that one of the corn silos looked a bit odd. I stood there for awhile, trying to figure out what was different, then I realized that what I was noticing was a kind of path going between the silo and the barn.

I walked over to where I could see better, and sure enough, there was a well-defined path with the snow all trampled and packed down. And this wasn't the path a fox or some small animal would make, but was more like something a human had worn down.

This worried me. Was someone living in the barn? If so, why would they be going to the silo? Could they get in? It really didn't make sense. But I didn't have time to check it out. I had to get to work.

Of course, I didn't get home until after dark again, and no way was I going out to investigate in the night. I'd have to wait until the weekend came. And when the weekend did come, it was snowing. And Sandy had to be gone at my aunt's all day.

Anyway, I mustered up the courage to go check everything out about early afternoon, after the snow had let up. I walked through the crusted snow out to the barn and carefully looked through a crack. There wasn't much light in there, and I didn't see anything, but I did notice a real strong musky odor. That led me to think there was indeed something or someone that had been staying in there.

I walked around to the front and noticed the door was unlatched. It actually had a big bar that went across the door, and the bar was down. This wasn't something that the wind might blow down, it was pretty sturdy. I was beginning to think we had a hobo or some homeless person staying there, and I felt a little sorry for them. It would be a hard life to live.

I lifted the bar back into place, firmly securing the big barn door.

The path to the metal corn silo was now drifted over a bit from the new snow, but I went ahead and walked over there. It was a good 50 feet away from the barn, over by two other silos, also filled with field corn.

What I saw was a bit of a shock. The silo door was open, and corn had spilled out. I looked inside, and it looked like half the corn was gone! I was stunned, but then I wondered if maybe it hadn't been partly empty in the first place.

Once again, the door had a latch, this one with a pin holding it in place, and the pin had been removed. I closed the door and set the pin, then walked around the other two silos, but nothing was amiss there. I went back inside, my feet now half-frozen and my pantlegs stiff.

I sat down by the big gas stove and took off my boots, then held my feet and hands to the fire. I thought about calling the sharecropper, but then decided not to. What would it accomplish? If the silo was being raided by something, it was too late now, what was done was done.

The farmer would just worry and possibly come out here to check it out, and what could he do? I knew he was waiting for the price to be high before selling. I decided the silo must've been half-empty. Even a hobo couldn't eat that much corn.

I took my mind off it all by making my specialty, home-made bread. Sandy would love that, and I would also make some baked beans and a salad to go with it for dinner.

When Sandy got home, I told her what I'd found. She sat there for a bit, silent. I knew she was thinking about that large dark thing she'd seen. Could this be what was raiding the silo? Was it living in the barn? It made us both kind of shiver.

The next day was Sunday, and I got up and went out to shovel the path through the yard to the cars. After I was done, I went back over to the barn. What I saw gave me the creeps.

The door had been pushed open, breaking the big board that held the door shut. Whatever did it had to be very strong, and it must have been inside when it did it, from the looks of the way the board was shattered. And the musky smell was now very strong.

On top of that, there were fresh tracks going to the silo, and once again they were big. And the silo door had been opened again. Whatever it was, it had to have hands to pull that pin out. And there was fresh corn spilling out!

I went back inside as quickly as possible. The place had now lost its comfy feeling, the little farmhouse out on the tallgrass prairie. For the first time, I wished we lived in town.

Sandy was gone again to Marie's, leaving me home all alone. I decided to call her and let her know what was going on. She wasn't too happy about the news and said maybe we should start looking for something to rent in town, even though we didn't want to abandon the farm, as who knew what vandals might break in.

When Sandy came home that night, she told me she actually ran up the walk to the house, she was that scared, even though the porch light was on. I didn't know what to say, as I'd been scared myself there all alone. And I'm a big guy.

Well, life seems to interfere with about everything, and we were both soon back to work and into our routines, trying to forget whatever it was in the barn. We both started looking around at rentals, but there just wasn't much. And we weren't sure how to handle leaving the farm. It didn't seem like a good idea.

So, things just went on as they were. The winter didn't get any better, even on into February. It was still bitter cold and snowy. I didn't bother to go check out the silo to see if the corn was disappearing, as I somehow knew it was. And I stayed away from the barn. Something about it gave me the creeps.

Sandy and I decided we'd just pay the sharecropper whatever the loss was. Maybe we were in denial, but no way did we want to go deal with the situation. I have no idea how we could have, anyway. Call the Sheriff? The Department of Wildlife? We decided to just try to ignore the problem. Not the best way to handle a situation, but in this case, it did end up being for the best.

I think whoever or whatever it was knew we were ignoring it on purpose, because it was very careful to not bother us, yet it didn't try to hide. As time went on, Sandy and I both caught glimpses of it, and it was then we knew it wasn't a person we were dealing with.

I saw it full-on once, and it was huge, black, and stood well over my head, and I'm 6'6". It was massive, covered in dark hair, with huge shoulders and penetrating eyes. It really scared me to death. Sandy saw it once, too.

By this time, we were both so uncomfortable being out there that we just spent most of our time in town. When I wasn't working, I'd go sit with my aunt until Sandy got off work, then we'd drive home together. It saved on gas, and we felt safer together.

My aunt really enjoyed having the company, which was good, as her health was rapidly deteriorating. We knew she didn't have much longer to live. We knew we'd have to get Hospice involved shortly, so we just tried to be there with her as much as we could.

About late March, I noticed the second silo had been opened. This was bad news for our pocketbook, but we ignored it.

Finally, it was spring. The snow was gone and the trees were greening up.

And of course, the inevitable happened, the sharecropper came out to get his corn. He'd sold it. The cattle feedlot was paying a premium price, since it was the tail-end of the season and supplies were low. Imagine his shock when he found not one, but two empty silos.

We told him what had happened. I was sure he'd be angry at our inability to address the situation, but he wasn't, especially when we told him we would eat the loss. And what he then told us gave us some perspective.

This creature had been in this area for years. It had been on every farm in the county at one time or another, stealing food and even the occasional chicken or turkey. It had been shot at, cussed at, and ignored, and it seemed that whoever had the bad luck to host it for the winter would eventually just give in, as nothing worked to chase the thing off. Nobody could bear to shoot it, as it looked too human.

We asked for more information, but all he said was we were dealing with a Bigfoot. We were shocked, yet it seemed to fit the profile and thereby answer our questions. And no, it had never harmed anyone. But a Bigfoot in Nebraska? Who would've guessed?

The sharecropper came back the next day with a loader and someone driving a truck and loaded up the remaining corn, such that is was, hauling it off.

Now the Bigfoot had nothing to eat, but the fields were green and the weather was nice. Surely it would now leave and seek some place a bit more promising, we hoped.

But it stayed. We knew this because it now took to coming around the house, as if seeking food. This made us both leery, and neither of us were at all inclined to walk around and enjoy the farm. We were kind of under house arrest, even if just in our own minds.

Before long, the sharecropper was back, ready to start preparing the fields for planting. He stopped by the house, and we talked a bit, then he went into the barn, where he'd stored his tractor and various implements. After a bit, he came back up to the house.

We talked some more. The barn stank to high heaven, and he was thinking about not renewing his lease this year. I could tell he was scared. Even though the creature had been around for a long time, and everyone had stories to tell about it, he had personally not had to deal with it until now, and he was having second thoughts. He said he would call soon and let us know his decision.

It was then that Sandy and I had the talk we'd both been avoiding since we first got there. What would we do with the farm when my aunt passed? She was now in Hospice care and it was only a matter of time, maybe a very short time.

When this situation had first transpired, I had thought we would maybe want to move permanently to the farm and make it our home. I was, of course, in the throes of nostalgia and recalling my good childhood times there, but now things were different.

The winter alone was enough to make us not want to stay, and this Bigfoot situation was becoming intolerable. The creature had now taken to coming right up to the kitchen window and looking in. Sandy had kind of encouraged this by feeding it scraps, but she of course had no idea how brazen it would get, she just felt sorry for it. She put up curtains.

We were both now scared to death. Can you imagine looking up and seeing a huge black head with a half-human face looking in at you? I was beginning to have nightmares nearly every night. Some nights it would come up and pound on the walls, and sometimes it would moan or make strange creepy noises. We both took to spending the night at my aunt's apartment whenever we could, both to be with her and to avoid the farm.

I called my brother and talked to him, and we decided to sell the place. I called the sharecropper and told him the news. He had decided not to farm there this year anyway, so he would come and get his equipment. I told him we'd pay our share of the corn when the farm sold. He had his stuff out of there within the week.

The days wore on, and when we were on the farm, Sandy fed the Bigfoot. I told her this was encouraging it to stay, but she's a very kind soft-hearted person, and as much as she hated seeing it and was scared of it, she felt sorry for it.

I think she was anthropomorphizing it, thinking of it as a person, whereas I considered it more of a monstrous beast. We argued over this, whether she should feed it, but she always won, and I decided it wasn't important, as we weren't there that much and would leave soon anyway. But to me, it was a monster, and I hated it.

We listed the place with a real-estate agent, a man who specialized in farms. He came out and put up a sign, and we soon had a few lookers.

In the meantime, my aunt passed away, and Sandy and I began dealing with closing down her apartment and selling her stuff, much of which was still on the farm. It was a big task, as she was a bit of a packrat, but we finally got on top of it.

We had decided to go back to Idaho, where our kids lived. We could use our share of the proceeds from the farm to buy a little place, or we might just bank it and use it for retirement. But we had to sell it first. We decided we needed to fix the little old farm house up a bit, nothing serious, just some fresh paint and that kind of thing, then we were going to leave.

The Bigfoot was still hanging around, and we wanted out. It now appeared to have set up housekeeping down by the little creek, as I found a nest down there one day while picking wild asparagus, one of the few days I had the courage to go outside. That was the end of the little bit of enjoyment I did have on the farm, as I was now too scared to ever go out.

Time wore on, and it was now June. This is the start of tornado season, and we began to keep an eye on the weather. When you live in tornado country, it just becomes second nature.

We were anxious to get out of there, now that we'd made up our minds. Plus, the apartment was no longer being rented, so we had no place to stay but the farm, and we definitely were not enjoying being there. We had pretty much done all we could, just some final things needed doing, then we would leave, probably in a week. We had both given our two-weeks' notice at work. We couldn't wait to be gone.

Then it happened. I will never forget this day as long as I live, nor will Sandy—it will be forever etched in our memories.

It was a Saturday, and we were both inside the house, doing some last-minute painting. Most of our stuff was packed into a U-haul trailer, in preparation for leaving, along with the antique furniture for our kids.

I had wondered if the Bigfoot knew what was going on. It was still coming up to the house every day, wanting food, and Sandy was obliging, leaving leftovers out for it on the back step. She would also buy things like day-old bread and apples.

We were both taking a break, drinking coffee and eating some homemade scones, when suddenly, I felt something hit the house like a ton of bricks. The whole house shook just a bit. Sandy and I both looked at each other, like what the heck? Then we heard the weirdest sound we've ever heard before or since. It started out as a moaning, then turned into an undulating shriek. Then something hit the house again.

We had no idea what was going on, but I did know the hair on the back of my neck was standing up, and I had a primal urge to flee, to run. I didn't know what to do, though, or where to run.

Sandy seemed to have her head on better than I did, and she ran to the window and looked out. She stood there for a moment, transfixed, then began to scream, "Run! Run! Get in the basement!" She grabbed my arm and practically dragged me down the stairs, just as I could hear a roaring sound like I've never heard before.

We got into the canning room, where my aunt had canned and stored vegetables from her garden, crouching down in the corner. Everything got deathly quiet, and I could feel the air pressure change. It became stuffy and hard to breathe. We then heard what can only be described as a hundred freight trains bearing down on us, and then we could hear wood splinting and things shattering. We held onto each other, both of us thinking we would soon die.

It was quickly over, but we continued to crouch down, as tornadoes can come over the same place more than once if they change direction. Sandy was softly weeping the whole time, and all I could do was hold her.

After awhile, we decided it was safe and went back upstairs, expecting to find the house totally destroyed, from the sound of it. We were half-shocked to find it still there, just as it was before, except with a few windows blown out. But we knew something had been seriously damaged, as we'd heard the sound ourselves. We hesitantly went outside.

The barn was completely gone. You would never have known there had been a barn there, and two of the silos were twisted masses of metal, thrown against a small grove of trees, while the third was completely missing. A small shed was also gone, and we never saw it again. A grove of trees to the west that had been planted as a windbreak was now gone, and not even stumps remained.

Our cars had not been touched, but the U-haul trailer was thrown onto its side, though it didn't appear to be damaged much. Later, we righted it with the help of a neighbor, and I hammered out the dent and all was well. Our stuff inside wasn't even hurt.

After the shock of it all, we both went back inside to recover, wondering how our neighbors had fared. We had no cell phone service, so we didn't know until later that the farm next to ours had been totally demolished, although no one was hurt, thankfully.

We left three days later, after I'd repaired the trailer and had the broken windows replaced. We couldn't wait to get out of there. I thought it would be hard to go, but it wasn't.

We drove across Nebraska and into Wyoming, then got a motel for the night. Sandy had been exceptionally quiet the whole trip, and I knew she was still in a bit of shock. I decided to take her out for a nice dinner at a kind of expensive restaurant and celebrate our luck in not getting hit by the tornado, as well as in getting out of Nebraska.

After dinner, we ordered some wine and, for the first time, Sandy talked about the incident. I asked her what she'd seen when she looked out the window, though I wasn't sure I wanted to know. I figured she'd seen the tornado—and maybe the Bigfoot. I had wondered what had hit the house, and why the Bigfoot was wailing like that.

What she told me made me very glad we had left, though later, when I thought about it some more, it actually made me very sad.

She had run to the window just in time to see the Bigfoot running from the house towards the barn, and she couldn't believe how fast it could run. It was terrified of something, but she didn't know what, as her range of vision wasn't that good from the house.

But just as the creature ran into the barn, she saw the tornado hit, and the barn was instantly nothing but flying debris, rotating in a circle on the outskirts of the twister. She saw a large black body flying through the air with the debris. That was when she realized what was going on and grabbed me and headed for the basement.

Sandy started crying. "You know, Joe," she added, "That creature probably gave its life for us. It must've seen the tornado coming and ran over to the house to warn us, slamming the side of the house. It then ran to the barn for shelter. I know it came up from the creek bottom to warn us, and if it had stayed down there, it would've been OK."

For the first time, I no longer considered the Bigfoot to be a monster. But, of course, it was then too late.

[16] Devil's Playground

This story came from a fellow called Baker. I don't know if that was his last name or his first, he just told us to call him Baker, so we did.

Some stories have a ring of authenticity, while others seem a bit far-fetched and it's listener beware. At first I thought this was one of the latter, but the more I think about it, I'm not so sure. Baker was part of a much older generation than most of my clients, and he had grown up in a different world. Who's to say that the Bigfoot's world back then wasn't also much different, more relaxed and happy with more of them around? —Rusty

I grew up on the river. That's what we called it, the river, but other people called it the Klamath River. Since we didn't ever travel, all we needed was to call it the river and everyone knew what we meant. It was a defining force in our lives.

You may think I'm talking about Oregon, but I'm not. I grew up in Northern California, not far from the little town of Happy Camp. I guess it is almost in Oregon, though—it's pretty dang close.

We lived on the river, and I mean almost literally on it. We were upriver from the town a bit, and you had to cross a swinging bridge to get to our worn-down ramshackle house, which set a bit above the river floodplain. You couldn't drive there, you had to park and walk across that swinging bridge, carrying your groceries or whatever you had. We had no electricity or running water, unless you count the river.

My parents had a guide business. My dad was a river guide, and he'd take fellows out fishing. They would just show up—it was all word of mouth back then. My mom provided the meals and hospitality and made sure people paid before they went out on the river. My sister and I, well, our job was to stay out of sight and out of trouble when my folks had clients, so we did.

We did that by running around like wild Indians and exploring the countryside. We knew that country better than most of the real Indians who lived there and still live there—it's the ancestral homeland of the Karuk.

The Marble Mountains are nearby, and they're a wild and rugged territory. We never went up there much, cause my parents were too busy with the fishing business. But my sister and I often would explore the foothills nearby, and we saw things that lived in the Marbles, things that came down to the lower country. Some of those things are not part of the scientific community's general outlook of what lives on Planet Earth, but we know they're out there.

If you know the area well, you may be familiar with what's called the Devil's Playground. I'm not even sure if they still call it that, but that's the name it came to be known by when I was growing up.

The Devil's Playground is a basin a few miles from where we lived on the river, and it's off the beaten path, way off. You can't get there by vehicle, although it may be that now days an ATV could get in there, they seem to be going about anywhere now. But when we were kids, you had to hike in there, a good three miles one-way. It didn't see too many people. There's a nice small lake there called Devil's Lake.

You know, I never used to give much thought to names like that, I figured whoever named the thing had a big imagination. You see devil's this or devil's that all over the country. But now I see things differently, and I wonder what happened there every time I see a name like that. Devil's Kitchen, Devil's Causeway, Devil Creek. I bet you can come up with a few yourself. Ever wonder what those devils were?

My sister Mandy and I discovered the Devil's Playground one summer day. We didn't know it was called that, and maybe it wasn't back then. If we had known, we probably would've stayed away, cause we'd seen enough to make us pretty leery and careful. Things like the big tracks down by the house that my parents tried to convince us were bears. But we knew better.

That area has a long history of Bigfoot. I can recall being really young and hearing about Bigfoot around the kitchen table.

I remember one story in particular, where my dad was talking to some guy who was a logger and was having trouble with Bigfoot coming into the logging camp and rolling huge 50-gallon barrels of fuel off the mountain. I grew up with these stories like some kids hear about little league.

So, my sister Mandy and I were always careful out there by ourselves exploring, we never strayed too far off—until we discovered Devil's Lake, that is. We had been told to get lost by out parents, so we did. We didn't really get lost, but nobody knew where we were except the two of us.

Now, you have to understand that back then, people didn't worry about their kids like they do now. It was completely normal for kids to run around, even little kids, and they were generally pretty safe. I won't get into the state of the world now, but my parents telling us to get lost was not a crime in any way. We were about nine and ten, so we weren't babies, and we already did a lot to contribute to the household, things like splitting wood and sewing and cooking. We weren't coddled and knew how to take care of ourselves.

So, Mandy and I packed ourselves a lunch and headed up a big nearby hill to take a look at the world. We huffed and puffed our way up there, then just sat and watched things transpire, people float down the river, birds fly by, clouds move along, that sort of thing.

We sat there and looked around and finally decided we wanted to climb a ridge in the distance. It seemed kind of risky, to go that far, it was at least two miles away, maybe more. But we had all day and nothing to do, so we took off. As you can guess, this was the ridge above Devil's Playground and Devil's Lake, though we didn't know that until we got there.

We took off and it didn't really take us all that long to get over there. We huffed and puffed up the hill, then, once on top, stood in awe at the beautiful little lake below us in the trees. It was a gem, sparkling in the sunlight, a deep blue.

We were tired, so we sat there, quietly eating our lunch.

After a bit, we got sleepy and napped.

I recall being awakened by something strange, a sound I wasn't at all familiar with. When you grow up out in nature like we did, your second sense is aware of everything around you, and I guess it must warn you, because this sure woke me up.

I lay there in the grasses for a minute, trying to place what I was hearing and wake up at the same time. I just couldn't figure it out, so I woke Mandy up.

We both sat up, then we both turned to the lake at the same time, where the sounds were coming from. We could immediately see what was going on, but it took awhile for our brains to process it.

We saw, down by the lake shore, what looked like a big picnic. There were people milling around, the grownups, while the kids were swimming in the lake, splashing and making all kinds of noise, obviously having a great time.

Only thing was, these weren't really people. We knew exactly what they were, but they weren't people. These were the first Bigfoot Mandy and I ever saw, and I can tell you, our jaws hit the ground. And to see that many at once, when most people have never seen even one, well, we felt pretty overwhelmed.

Mandy, being the smarter one, wanted to immediately leave, and actually, so did I, but my curiosity also kicked in. I talked her into staying for just a few minutes. How often did one get to see what looked like a Bigfoot picnic? It was eerie and creepy and scary and fun all at once, watching those giant beasts milling around while the kids played in the water. It was an overwhelming sight.

I counted 14 adults and 12 children of all sizes. There were even two Bigfoot babies being carried around. Of course, we were a good quarter-mile or so above them, but we could plainly see them, although the features weren't very visible. They looked like giant humans all in shades of black and brown, with two of them having gray highlights. Maybe they were grandparents, we thought.

The Bigfoot children swam and played just like human kids would, and the adults seemed to be visiting, just like adult humans. They appeared to be talking to each other. This is what woke me up.

Now Mandy was getting scared and wanted to leave. She was starting to cry, so we stood up and started back down the hill.

We practically ran all the way home, totally spooked by what we had seen. Yes, it was a rather pastoral scene, until you stopped and thought about what you were looking at, that is. I remember that neither of us wanted to go outside much after that, and it really put a damper on our explorations.

Our parents noticed, of course, and wanted to know why. What had happened to turn us into homebodies? We finally told them, thinking they would get mad at us for going so far from home and also maybe accuse us of lying. They were shocked, and I'm not sure they did believe us.

But not long afterwards, my dad came home one day and told us we were moving. He had a new job, one in the Sierras, up by the little town of Twain Harte. It was a whole new lifestyle, as he'd taken a job helping run a ranch. We would live in a little house on the ranch and have electricity and running water.

It wasn't until years later, when I asked my mom about it one day while we were visiting and got the truth.

Not long after we'd been up there, Mom and Dad had decided to go see the lake for themselves. Others had seen strange things there, and my parents wanted to know what was going on practically in their back yard. They hiked up the same hill we had, but they hadn't seen anything, no Bigfoot picnic on Devil's Lake. Nothing.

But as they turned to hike back, something started following them, breathing heavily, something they knew was a Bigfoot just from the sound of its weight on the ground as it walked parallel to them in the trees, hidden in the undergrowth and thick foliage.

My dad panicked. My mom held his hand and talked him into not running, telling him to just keep walking slow and steady. They finally got out of the trees and came back home, but that thing followed them clear to the edge of the forest, which wasn't all that far from the house.

That was it. They were afraid for us and also for themselves.

So, we moved into the California Gold Country and began new lives. Ironically, Twain Harte is a hotbed of Bigfoot activity—there have been many sightings there over the years, maybe more than up near Happy Camp. But we stayed, leading much more normal lives, for better or worse. And when my parents finally retired, guess where they went to live?

You guessed it—Happy Camp. They missed their friends and the river. But they didn't move out into the country—they stayed right in town.

[17] The Bigfoot Wedding

This story was told by a retired guy who had learned to love flyfishing and wanted to have a pro show him some of the ropes. He came on a three-day guided trip and told this crazy story around a big campfire up in Montana's Yellowstone River country. That particular trip was a lot of fun, and he became a regular after that, coming on one of my trips every year. He was always game to tell this story, and it was quite the tale. —Rusty

My name is Tanner, and what I'm about to relate happened in the mid-1990s, maybe about 1996, in Telluride, Colorado.

I grew up near Telluride, and I was a true ski bum for a number of years. I would do anything to ski, which included sleeping (i.e., freezing) in my car, working in ski rental shops, couch surfing, washing dishes, you name it. Anything so I could ski, which I loved.

I finally got on the ski patrol there, which was a dream job in some ways, though the pay wasn't that great. A bunch of us rented a three-bedroom apartment and managed to get by. I think there were six of us living there, and

I got the couch for reduced rent. But we didn't care where we lived, we were all ski bums.

I gradually decided I should move on and get some job skills, so I left Telluride when I was in my late twenties and moved to Grand Junction, where I got a career job with the Department of Wildlife. That was great, because I was still outside a lot, but now I had some job security and a decent wage. I stayed there until I recently retired.

But this event happened in Telluride, and I've never seen anything like what I saw that day, even though I'm outside a lot. In a way, it's kind of funny, though at the time I was terrified.

I had managed to wrangle a job that summer with the ski area, working as a lift operator. It was a pretty cushy job, though like ski patrolling, it didn't pay much. I ran the Coonskin Lift, the one that comes right up out of town. I think it's still operating, though I know they've added the gondola now, too. But in the summer, it was just a tourist thing and you didn't get all the crazy skiers who fall when they're getting on and off, making you have to stop everything all the time. So, running Coonskin in the summer was pretty easy—usually, anyway.

I was working the ski shack at the top of the lift, where everyone gets off to either ski back down or go to the next lift, although in the summer everyone was obviously hiking. The altitude at the shack was 10,800 feet.

If I recall correctly, it was late July, the time the monsoons start to hit the area. Colorado mountain weather is pretty nice in June, but come mid-summer, the monsoons hit, which means lots of rain and lightning. Usually, the mornings are nice, but by afternoon, you'd better be off the mountains.

So, I was running the lift, and everything was fine, just a typical day with a few hikers and sightseers. It wasn't too busy, and I managed to grab some lunch while running the lift.

It wasn't long after lunch that my boss showed up to inform me that we were getting a huge bunch of people soon because there was a wedding at the top of the mountain. I was to be extra careful, as some of these people would be older and not in such great shape, and I might have to slow the lift down for them to get off. And on top of that, they'd all be in fancy wedding attire, with high heels and all that. Some big star of the Miami Dolphins, a fullback, was getting married.

Great. I couldn't wait. A bunch of dressed-up city folk trying to ride the Coonskin Lift, which was very steep and scary. Make my day. I started laughing, but my boss got kind of tense and said this was serious. He knew I could be a smart-ass, and he knew that big money was something to be respected in Telluride, at least every one else seemed to think so—everyone except the crowd I ran with, that is. I stopped laughing, but I couldn't wipe the grin off my face. All those people dressed to kill and dangling from a ski lift.

My boss decided to stick around and make sure everything went well. It was a big wedding party, about 300 people, a big responsibility for him. I guess he decided he needed to handle it, as I wasn't competent enough, even though I'd been running the lift alone for over a month by then.

Well, it wasn't long before people started showing up. I don't know what the Coonskin Lift capacity is, but I think we had all 300 people on it when what I'll call "the Event" happened.

So, picture a very steep and scary ski lift, the kind with only a bar across the front to hold you in, all crammed with uppity-dressed people, tuxes and high heels and crazy long dresses and even hats and all. Man, I wish I'd had a camera, cause just that alone was something I'd never seen before or since. It belonged in a movie.

Of course, it took awhile to get everyone onto the lift. One chair would come into place, then the lift would stop while people boarded, then the same thing would happen again. I was at the top, like I said, but I could tell what was happening from how the lift went. I knew it would take a long time to get everyone off when they got up to my lift shack.

So, during all this, which was a while, I was noticing the sky was getting dark. Clouds were moving in really fast, which is typical for the mountains. My boss was also noting the same thing, and he started looking even more tense. Usually, when the clouds came in, we would just shut the lift down until it all moved through, but no way could we do that with what was going on.

Everything seemed to take forever. Getting all these people on the lift was a big deal. I watched as cloud tendrils began wrapping around the higher peaks. Holy crap, I thought, we could be in for a wild ride.

Finally, the lift stopped stopping, and I knew everyone was loaded on. Sure enough, here they came. I could see down the slope and the entire lift was loaded to the gills. There was a huge variety of people, from young to old. Some looked like they were scared to death and some were laughing and having a great time. The lift began its slow upward climb just as lightning started popping all around the upper peaks.

Man, that lift seemed like it was going even slower than normal, but I knew it was just because I wanted it to go fast and get up here before anyone got smacked by lightning. Before long, the lightning was popping all around us.

This is when the Event happened. My boss and I were both in the lift shack, and he had his hands on the lift mechanism, ready to stop it whenever the first passengers arrived. They were now about two-thirds of the way up the hill.

I was looking out the open door at the peaks above me, watching the lightning, when I heard a weird noise come from my boss—it was literally a scream, if you can imagine a grown man screaming. It scared the crap out of me, and I turned to see what was going on. He was pointing to the lift shack window, but I didn't see anything. He then started kind of babbling while he pointed at the window.

I stepped out of the shack to see what was going on, and that was when I saw it. By then it had turned and was loping down the steep hill. I think my boss scared it as much as it scared my boss, cause it wasn't wasting any time. And it was running directly down the Coonskin Run, right under the big wedding party.

I knew immediately what it was—a Bigfoot. I'd never seen one or even thought of seeing one before—Bigfoot wasn't much of a big deal in Colorado at that time. Since then, there have been more and more sightings, maybe because there are more people out and about, I don't know. But it was a sight that's etched into my memory, the backside of a Bigfoot, running down Coonskin. The creature was enormous and very dark, covered head to toe in what looked like black hair—not fur like a bear would have—but hair. The hair was long and hung off its arms, which themselves hung down almost to its knees.

I couldn't believe how fast this thing was. It was running down Coonskin faster than any Miami Dolphin fullback could possibly run. That thing was moving!

As I came back into the lift shack, I noticed my boss had a glazed look on his face, but he was also kind of gesticulating at me as if trying to say something. I think the poor guy was in shock at that point.

I quickly noticed what was going on. He'd slammed the lift bar when he saw the Bigfoot and the lift was now going at top speed. Oh man, this was bad, real bad, cause I knew it was going to jump track at that speed with that much weight on it.

Sure enough, all of a sudden it stopped with a lurch, the chairs swaying back and forth and people yelling. It was such a stunning chain of events, I almost started shaking.

Here we were, lightning now popping all around, with an inoperative lift crammed with people dressed for a wedding, many of who were now screaming and yelling as they witnessed a Bigfoot running directly under where they now sat dangling in the air. What a scenario.

My boss was now sitting helplessly on the floor, so I took over. I went outside and yelled up at the people closest to me to pass the word down the lift that help was coming. Of course, it wasn't, not yet, anyway, but the last thing we needed were people panicking, many who didn't want to even be on that lift in the first place, especially with lightning popping around.

So, I could hear people yelling the message on down the line. I went back into the shack and radioed down to the bottom that we needed help. Before long, I saw an ATV coming up the slope. By now, the Bigfoot had decided to head into the trees and was long gone, leaving only a residue of terror and bafflement. I think a lot of people thought it was some kind of a gag.

It now started to pour rain. The guys on the ATV were soon climbing up the lift tower where the derailment had happened, checking it out. Those guys should've got commendations for taking their lives in their hands, cause now the lightning was just crazy. I saw and heard one bolt at the same time, it was that close.

They were up there for some time, then came back down and on up to the shack, where they informed me that we were going to have to evacuate everyone off the lift. There was no way they could get it back on track.

This would be a slow and treacherous process, especially with so many people involved. They radioed down, and soon people working for the ski area starting coming up the slope. I think there were probably a good 50 or 60 people there helping before it was all over, including a search and rescue team.

The ski people brought a bunch of bosun's chairs with them that the ski area kept just for this purpose. These little chairs were lightweight and attached to the end of a rope. If you were stuck on the lift, the M.O. was to get hold of the bosun's chair and sort of scoot it under you until you were well in it, then you latched yourself in and were lowered by whoever was holding the end of the rope.

So, we now had to throw the bosun's chairs over the cable to lower people down with. You would take the chair and start spinning it around your head until it got up a lot of momentum, then you'd hurl it as hard as you could, hoping it would go up over the lift cable.

Once you had it over, you were home free, cause then you could use it over and over to lower people. We had a minimum of three people holding each rope, acting as a belay while each person was lowered. The person on the lift would slip the chair under them, then when they were ready, they'd wave or yell at us, and we'd then yell "on belay!" and start lowering them, one by one.

Many were terrified of getting on the spindly looking chairs, as the height was really scary, and I didn't blame them. We had several people who refused to even get into the chairs, but we persuaded them by saying it was that or spend the night and who knows how long on the chair lift. That would finally get them moving, but I mean they were scared stiff.

As for those of us on the belay end, holding the ropes, it was steep terrain and hard to stand up, especially with a rope around your waist and some scared person on the other end, being lowered little by little. It took us four hours to get them all off the lift.

By then, the rain had stopped and the storm moved on through, but everyone was still soaked. It was amazing no one was hit by lightning.

The ski area had to do something with all these soaked and unhappy people, so they hired the local taxi service to come up. Telluride Taxi had Suburbans at the time, and they drove up the Coonskin snowcat trail to pick everyone up. The ski area was billed later for this, and I bet it cost them a fortune.

By the time it was all over, my boss had recovered somewhat and hiked on back down Coonskin Run without saying one word to me. He told me later that he'd seen this black thing staring in through the shack window at him, no more than ten feet away, with a large dark face almost like a human's. When I told him that I and everyone on the lift had also seen it, I think it helped a bit. Maybe he wasn't crazy after all.

After it was all over, I just stood there, kind of enjoying it all, watching all these people walking in the wet grass in their soaked wedding duds, a lot of the women barefoot, as they'd taken off their heels. It seems the majority were kind of having fun, enjoying the adventure, but some people looked outright shocked, mostly the older ones. But everyone was talking about the Bigfoot. I think by then everyone thought it was just a big gag someone had contrived for their enjoyment. A few looked really uncomfortable, like they were sure it was real.

By the time it was over, it was nearly sunset. The taxis were long gone, so I had to get myself home. I normally would ride the lift down, but now I had to hike down. I didn't want to hike down Coonskin, as I was pretty scared by the thought of a Bigfoot around, so I hiked over to the Plunge and came down that way. I was glad when I got into town, and I went home and told my buddies about what had happened. They believed me, so they said, anyway.

I found out later that the Bigfoot story was soon all over town, and I'd become somewhat of an accidental celebrity. I kind of ran with it for awhile, as it was all in fun, resulting in some free beer and lots of questioning—all in fun if you hadn't seen the creature and been scared to death, that is.

And in all honesty, I had been scared to death. I didn't do much hiking at all that summer, and when I was out, I was always looking over my shoulder. I was the last one to operate the Coonskin lift during the summer, as the Gondola went online that year, and the Coonskin lift is now only open during the winter.

What was a Bigfoot doing on Coonskin? I think it was hungry and was attracted to the big plastic trash bins up by the snack shack, only about 50 feet above the lift shack. I saw a brown bear up there one day, just mulling around through the trash, and I know they threw a lot of food away in there.

By the time winter came, I was fine, figuring the beast had probably gone somewhere else for the cold season, so I was back on the slopes skiing like a madman. And it was the only time I ever heard of a Bigfoot there, so maybe, like me, it was just wondering what in the heck was going on that wedding day.

[18] Camping with Uncle Hairy
· ·

I get a number of Utah anglers who come over to Colorado to learn the fine art of fly-tying, and this story was told by one such person. I wish I could tell it like Seth, the storyteller, did—he had us all on pins and needles. I think he relived some of the terror while telling this story, as he was real quiet after that. Hang on for a wild ride! —Rusty

My cousin Terry had become pretty interested in Bigfoot ever since his son said he'd seen one near their home in Sevier, Utah. This is the story of how I got involved in his so-called research, which turned out to be a bit more than either of us bargained for.

I'm Seth, and I know you're probably going to think I'm lying because this story is so crazy, but I want you to know that after it all happened, I went to the nearest police station (Richfield) and filed a report, something I've never done before. In my mind, it was serious enough I thought they should know. And I also thought it might save the next guy from being laughed at if they already had my report on record and someone else came in. They probably laughed at me, but that's OK.

I live in Salt Lake City, but my family's from the Sevier Valley, which lies along the western flanks of the Wasatch Plateau, though my side of the family left there when I was a kid. This is not to be confused with the Wasatch Mountains, near Salt Lake, but is a big plateau in central Utah.

It's pretty much rugged country that's used only by the occasional hunter and a few cattleman running a few head of stock. I bet there are places in there that haven't seen a human since the Native Americans lived there, unless it would be a bow hunter.

Well, Terry's son Jared, my nephew, came running into their house one day saying he'd seen a Bigfoot. They live near Sevier, an old ranching community at the foot of the plateau. Terry just laughed, but when he realized Jared was white as a sheet, he went out and investigated and found some tracks. They never saw the thing again, but this was the start of Terry's obsession, and I guess mine, too.

Terry started reading everything he could on the internet and even talked around town to see if anyone else had seen one. He managed to hook up with a bow hunter who told him he'd been followed by a Bigfoot up on the plateau one time.

Terry got the location, called me, and we decided to go for an outing up there and see what we could find. Of course, I didn't even believe in Bigfoot or I would've been too scared to go off looking for them. I thought it was kind of a big joke and something fun to do.

I have a pickup with a camper on it, so I loaded it up with all my gear and headed south for Terry's. I had a four-day weekend. I got to his place and we loaded up his gear, then went to the grocery store and got supplies. I thought for sure his son Jared would be coming along, but he wanted nothing to do with it. In fact, he had tried to talk his dad out of going.

I guess his encounter really shook him up and he had no intention of seeing another one. That kind of made me pause—what if these darn things were real?

We headed out, climbing up a dirt road that paralleled Interstate 70, going back up on the Wasatch Plateau. I think it was called Gooseberry Road. After a bit, it left the freeway and headed out into the backcountry, winding through a small valley and then up on top.

We were going to camp at this spot that Terry knew up in the aspen trees. It was near a place where rockhounds went to look for septarian nodules, a kind of sandstone ball that you can cut in two and the interior has a beautiful pattern like a tree trunk with branches. They're pretty rare, and this was one of the few places they're found. If we got bored, we could look for nodules, and maybe sell a few to the local rock shop in Sevier.

The road wound up and up along a gentle slope, and it wasn't long before we were up where we wanted to camp. It was a pretty little clearing in the aspens with plenty of shade and grasses. There wasn't another soul anywhere to be seen. I pulled the truck around to where the camper door opened into the clearing, then Terry unloaded his gear.

He had a big cabin tent, and we set that up, complete with his cot, lantern, and everything else. There was a fire pit there from previous campers, so I set the camp chairs by it and went and started gathering some wood while Terry finished setting up his camp.

Man, that tent was nice. It was almost as big as my bedroom back home, and it had nice big screened-in windows that really made it almost like being outdoors. He then put up a big mosquito-net room that attached to the front of the tent. If the skeeters got bad, we could move our chairs in there.

Of course, the first thing you always want to do after you pitch your tent is kick back and have a beer or coffee or whatever it is you drink. I'm preferential to coffee, so I fired up the stove in my camper and made some hot java. Terry drank some iced-tea from a big gallon milk jug he'd brought along.

It was only mid-afternoon, so we decided to go look for nodules. We got our rock hammers out and headed down the hill a bit, where there was a rock outcropping. We could see where people had dug into the cliffside, leaving small pits everywhere. The outcropping followed this small drainage for quite some ways, so we hiked back a bit, looking for new areas that hadn't been all dug up. We spent most of the afternoon messing around there, but finding only a few small nodules.

That was actually a lot of fun, in a mellow hanging out kind of way, and before we knew it, the sun was setting over the valley rim. We hoofed it back to camp, carrying the nodules in our pockets. We made a small pile of them next to the truck. We'd crack them open later and see what was inside. If we found anything nice, Terry would take them home and polish them up and take them to the rock shop. I guess when you get to be a middle-aged geezer, rock hounding is attractive cause you can be outdoors and be lazy but still feel like you're doing something.

It was now dusk, and we decided to have some dinner. All that hard work had made us hungry. Terry had brought some steaks, so we put those on the grill over a small campfire. I pulled out some potato salad and stuff we'd bought earlier at the store. By the time everything was ready, it was fairly dark. I put some logs on the fire and we pulled our chairs up close and ate.

I don't know what it is about sitting around a campfire, but it always seems to bring out talk of the philosophical and mysterious. We sat there after dinner, drinking beer and talking about everything under the sun—from the meaning of life to UFOs—and then the talk turned to Bigfoot. Terry wanted to talk about Bigfoot. I thought, well, OK, he's the one sleeping in the tent, so if it doesn't bother him, I guess we're OK.

Before long, Terry was telling me some of the stories he'd read on the internet. He went on to describe what the typical Bigfoot looked like and how it acted and all that. He then related a few encounters he'd read about in this general area, one where some people were harassed in their camp trailer, not too far from where we were currently camped, and another way up on the northern end of the plateau where some hunters had been stalked.

After a bit, I had to go relieve myself. I stepped away from the fire into the darkness. I hadn't seen stars like that for many years—the whole sky was just hanging with them. It was as if you could reach up and touch them. But as I stood there, a real spooky sense came over me, and it was all I could do to not panic. I was soon back by the fire.

In the meantime, Terry had decided it would be cool to do some wood knocking and see if there was anything out there that would reply. He told me that this is how Bigfoot communicate their locations to each other—they knock on trees with big sticks of wood.

By this time, I was pretty spooked. By daylight, I didn't believe in Bigfoot. I mean, if they were real, surely someone would come up with some real evidence, the kind you take to a lab—a body or something. But sitting out here far from civilization in the dark, they suddenly became a very real possibility. I didn't want to have anything to do with bringing them into our camp, and I told Terry that.

I think he was surprised, but he seemed pretty spooked himself and agreed it might not be so much fun to have these big guys around our camp in the dark. He joked that the smell of the steaks had probably already informed them of our presence, and they'd be coming around soon without us having to do any wood knocking. I told him I hoped not, but since he was the one in the tent, to let me know in the morning.

By then, I was pretty tired, so I said goodnight and climbed into the camper. He was going to sit by the fire a bit longer, then he would put it out and go to bed himself.

I crawled into bed and lay there for a bit. I'm a bit claustrophobic and can't sleep up over the cab, so I always use the dining area bed. As I lay there, I thought about the quiet. There's nothing like the quiet you hear out in the wilds, or maybe I should say, all the stuff you don't hear. But it finally dawned on me that this place had absolutely no night sounds of any kind, not even crickets, which usually seem to be everywhere. It was odd and a bit ominous.

I finally drifted off, kind of wishing I had Brandy here with me, my wife's little Cairn Terrier. I laughed at myself. What could a little dog like that do if a Bigfoot came around? Maybe not much, but they were good on the early warning end of things. Hell, I was even wishing I had my somewhat fussy wife with me, which isn't really what macho men out in the wilderness typically wish for. I finally drifted off.

I woke up sometime in the night and tossed and turned, not able to go back to sleep. I could see the fire out my little side window, and it was still going great guns. I could see Terry's form in the shadows cast by the fire. He was still sitting there. I looked at my watch—11 p.m. I'd climbed into the camper a mere hour ago. I was tired—why couldn't I sleep? And how long was he going to stay up? He would run out of wood soon, I thought, and then have to go to bed.

I must have drifted off again, because when I next woke up, light was streaming into the camper window. I lay there for a bit, then got up and stuck my head out the door. Nobody around, Terry must still be sleeping. I made some coffee, then took it outside and sat by the now-cold ashes in the fire ring.

It was a beautiful morning with a bluebird sky and a few white wispy clouds. All the spookiness of last night was gone, and I wondered why I'd been so scared. Chalk it up to the power of the human imagination.

Before long, Terry was up and about, and I offered him some coffee. We both sat there and talked a bit about the previous night. He had sat up for a couple of hours, kind of afraid to put the fire out and go to bed, but he finally got so tired he had no choice.

We both kind of laughed about how spooked we'd been, then made some breakfast and decided to drive a few miles up to a small lake and do some fishing. We still had a couple of days before we had to go back, and we wanted to make the most of them.

Well, I can say that day was one of the finest days of my life. It was so quiet and peaceful up there, and just hanging around that little lake with nobody in sight except Terry, just enjoying the beauty of nature, well, it was just really great.

But when we drove back down to where the tent was, well, that was the end of that peaceful feeling.

Someone had stolen Terry's nice cabin tent! They had taken the whole thing, along with its contents—the cot, his sleeping bag, everything. That tent cost Terry a good sum, close to a thousand dollars, as it was a nice outfitter's tent. Our other stuff, the camp chairs, our grill, a lantern, and a few odds and ends were all just as we'd left them.

We'd been at the lake all day, and it was now dusk, but we walked around, trying to see if we could make sense of anything, maybe find some boot tracks. Terry was over by where his tent had been, looking at the ground, when he whistled for me to come over.

We both stood there and looked at marks on the ground that led into the nearby aspens. It looked like someone had actually dragged the tent off! We started following the drag marks. Whoever did it must've had help, cause that tent was big and heavy, and it had all kinds of Terry's camp gear in it.

The marks went quite a ways from the clearing, way over onto the next hill. My God, whatever dragged that tent that far was strong! We didn't see any tracks because of the grasses. We finally found the tent, just when we were about ready to turn back because of the failing light. There it lay in a heap, one side completely torn off. Who was strong enough to just rip heavy canvas apart like that? Terry's cot and gear were all still in the tent. We got what we could out, and headed back. No way were we going to drag that tent back, it would take some doing, and it was almost dark.

We made it back to camp, both of us looking over our shoulders all the way. We were now beginning to realize that whatever had taken the tent was big and probably angry at our presence. We knew it wasn't a bear, as they don't have hands to drag things like that. We didn't talk about what it could be, but we knew.

By then, we were starving, as we hadn't eaten since having some sandwiches at lunch. I immediately built a fire, but we hadn't collected more wood, and our supply was low. I got the rest of our steaks from my camper fridge and started them cooking on the stove in the camper. Terry was now just sitting by the fire, looking like he was in shock.

I went out and sat by him. We talked about what we should do. It was now dark. He could spend the night in my camper, sleeping up above the cab, and then we could go get the tent in the morning and see if it was salvageable and worth the trouble of dragging it back. But in all honesty, I just wanted to leave. I knew he did, too, but he was torn, as he didn't want to leave that expensive tent up here. I told him we should leave and come back for it tomorrow, as it wasn't that far of a drive.

We went inside and had dinner, not sure what to do, but knowing what we wanted to do. Why didn't we leave? I don't know. We were both really tired and our common sense wasn't working, I guess. And being inside the camper made things a bit less scary.

We sat there and talked for a bit, trying to unwind.

Finally, the topic came around to what could have taken the tent, a subject we'd both kind of been avoiding. It was then that Terry started telling me about the little town of Marysvale, not that far away as the crow flies, over by the tourist trap called the Big Rock Candy Mountain. Near Marysvale is a canyon called Gorilla Canyon. He said the locals refused to go there and wouldn't talk about it. We're talking a bit of a ways from our camp, but not terribly far. To me, it was more evidence that these creatures inhabited the area and that we should leave.

Before long, the food kicked in, and we were both so tired we were nodding off, so we went to bed. We'd get up first thing, get the tent, then leave.

I slept like a log until sometime in the middle of the night when I woke, thinking I was in an earthquake. The truck was rocking back and forth so hard I thought it would tip over any second. I could barely get to my feet. Terry was trying to climb out of the overhead bed and ended up falling pretty much on top of me. I started yelling at him that we should get out of the truck when all of a sudden, the action stopped.

We regrouped, sitting on the bench bed, sure we'd been in an earthquake. We were a bit shocked. I turned on an inside light.

Shortly after, something slammed against the side of the truck, hard. It was like someone huge had slapped it with their open hand. Holy crap, this was no earthquake!

Now someone was fiddling with the door handle, trying to get it open. I had locked it before going to bed, but whoever it was, they were about to twist the handle off!

I started yelling at them to get the hell out of here or I would shoot them. Of course, I didn't have a gun, but I thought it might deter them.

Terry looked at me and just said calmly, "I doubt if they understand English."

It was then that it really hit me what was out there, and I felt the blood rush to my head, and I was dizzy for a minute.

The handle was straining under the force and would go any minute. What could we do? We could now hear a moaning sound, and it made my blood run cold. I was suddenly chilled.

Terry was now cussing. I think he had more presence of mind than I did. I kept the pickup keys hanging on a little knob on the kitchen cupboard, and he grabbed them. I was now scared stiff, thinking he was going to try to go out the door and get into the cab, but instead, he opened the little window in the camper that led into the cab and crawled though it. There was no way I could follow him, as I'm too big.

I could hear the truck start, and then it jerked forward as Terry put it into first and took off. Everything in the back clanked and rolled around, as I still had the cooking stuff out and hadn't battened down the hatches. I myself was nearly tossed off the bench seat.

Now something slammed against the truck again, and I could hear the crunching sound of something big running alongside us, exactly next to where I was sitting. What I did next I will always regret, although in some ways I had to know. I leaned against the side of the camper and carefully pulled the curtain aside just enough so I could see out.

It was dark enough that all I could make out was a dark form running beside us, having no trouble at all keeping up, although by now Terry was really pushing it, bumping and careening down the rough narrow dirt road.

This thing's shoulder was about equal to the window, and that meant it was huge. But now I could see its giant arm grabbing onto the camper tie-down in the front corner, and it was now wrenching it off.

Holy crap! If it managed to pull the camper off the truck, I was history. I was now terrified. Terry had told me that Bigfoot was a gentle giant—yeah, right! I could now feel the camper bouncing where that corner was no longer anchored.

I started screaming at Terry to go faster, telling him it was trying to tear the camper off! He was already going dangerously too fast for that back road, and I knew if he lost control, that would be it for both of us. If we didn't get hurt in the crash, who knows what the Bigfoot would do to us!

I pulled the curtain back just a little once more to see what was going on, though I could barely stay in the seat. Two glowing red eyes met mine, just inches away. It was looking inside, and it knew I was right there. I jumped, pulling the curtain back in place and diving for the floor, where I stayed the entire way back.

Terry must've hit a flat straight stretch of road, cause he was now really hauling, making good time. Again, the Bigfoot slapped the side of the truck. He was still right there! How could this thing run that fast?

Now I could feel the back tie-down being ripped away from the other side. I later realized that if that creature had torn off the back one on the same side as the front one he'd taken off earlier, I wouldn't have made it back, as the camper would've tipped off when Terry took those curves so fast.

I have never been so terrified in my life. I thought I was going to die, and it wasn't like thinking you're going to die in a close-call car wreck or something like that. The sheer terror of it all made everything magnified a million times. I could never adequately explain it, words simply don't work.

Terry was going even faster, and I then heard the most chilling sound—the Bigfoot was now behind us, and it was screaming! The sound went on and on and still haunts my dreams. But it was falling behind, and I knew we had managed to escape. How Terry kept his wits enough to drive like that, I'll never know.

It didn't take all that long to get back to Terry's house, maybe an hour. I just lay there on the floor the entire time. I felt the truck stop and the engine go quiet, but I couldn't get up. Terry had to climb into the camper and help me to my feet. We both went inside the house, where I just lay down on the couch and passed out. The last thing I recall is Terry locking all the doors as his wife asked him what was going on.

The next day, we assessed the damage to my truck. I had to get new tie-downs and have them installed by the local RV place, where I endured some teasing about going too fast on rough roads.

They also had to patch the camper corners where the tie-downs had been ripped out, and this cost me some cash, as it took some major work to repair the holes. There were also a couple of dents where the creature had slammed my truck with his huge hands. I just left those for later.

I wasn't able to go home for a couple of days, but that was OK. I needed to stay there with Terry and rehash the whole thing. We talked about it over and over until we had covered every possible detail and angle. We were both in shock.

Terry's wife and son were fascinated by our story and seemed to fully believe it. His wife is the one who encouraged us to go to the sheriff and report it. Who knows what they did with that information, but we thought maybe it would help if someone else ever saw it, too.

I finally went home, glad to be back in the city for the first time in my life. As far as I know, Terry's tent is still up there where the Bigfoot left it, the canvas probably rotting in the summer rains, a testament to forces much bigger and more mysterious than one could ever imagine. I'm sure someone eventually found our septarian nodules.

And as far as I know, Terry never went Bigfoot hunting again.

[19] The Crybaby

. . . .

This story happened in my home stomping grounds of North-west Colorado, but that's not where I first heard it. People here still talk about it, as the storyteller wasn't the only one in these parts who had an encounter with this mysterious and very vocal creature.

I first heard this story while visiting an old fishing buddy down in Salida, Colorado. The storyteller was my buddy's wife, but she was hesitant to tell it to a relative stranger until my friend told her I collected Bigfoot stories and was a believer. After telling the story, we had a long talk about the creature, and it seemed to help, as she said she hadn't met many people who believed her. —Rusty

I was visiting my sister one summer for a few weeks when this crazy incident occurred. I'll never forget it, even if I get Alzheimer's someday, it was that traumatic.

I'm Sandy, and my sister Katy is a few years older than me. She had finished college and was married and living in Steamboat Springs, Colorado, a resort ski town. I was still in college over in Boulder, and I liked to go visit her on breaks.

She and her husband had bought a nice house at the foot of Emerald Mountain in a sort of working-class subdivision, though it was nice. The house kind of set on the lower flanks of the mountain, above the town. She and her husband and kids have since moved to Craig, down the road an hour or so, where the climate isn't quite so snowy. They have a physical therapy business there.

So, one summer break I wanted to see my sister and also get out of the city, so I went on over to Steamboat. I would guess this happened in about 2005, not all that long ago, really. I hope nobody since then has had this happen to them. My sister said she'd never heard anything like it.

Emerald Mountain is this big mountain that has slopes that are steep, but not overly so, one can hike them. It's pretty big, but I consider it more of a giant hill than a mountain, as it's not like some of the nearby mountains like Mount Werner. It has some big open meadows—one is shaped like a heart—and lots of scrub oak and aspen trees, then pines up higher. If you drive around its backside, there are some houses and ranches there, but it's pretty much wild terrain.

It belongs to the city and the BLM, and there are a bunch of hiking trails up there, as well as an old road to a former quarry.

When I was there, you could just kind of take off from the end of the subdivision and hike up as far as you wanted and there was nobody or anything around, no fences. It was really like being in the wilderness far from anything, but yet close to home. I liked to go up there with my sister's dog, Smoky, a big gray mutt, because I could let him run and not worry about other dogs being around like on the hiking trails.

So, one day, after I'd been there a couple of weeks, I decided to go a bit further out and make it more of an outing. I packed a little daypack with water for me and Smoky and some snacks and headed out. I'd guess it was about 10 a.m.

We climbed up the mountain, following a deer trail through the scrub oak and up into the aspens. Once you got into the trees, the going was much easier, as it was mostly grasses and wildflowers interspersed with white-barked aspens.

We were having a great time. After about an hour or so, we sat on some big rocks and had lunch, which consisted of a granola bar for me and a few dog biscuits for Smoky. We'd climbed up quite a bit and could see out. I could see the town far below and the flanks of the ski area in the distance to the east. We just hung out there for a long time, watching the magpies and clouds and enjoying being out.

But all of a sudden Smoky started acting funny. He wasn't on a leash, and he got up and acted like he was listening to something for a bit, then he started whining. He then came up to me and kind of nosed my leg, then turned and started walking back down the mountain. He turned around to see if I were following, and when he saw I wasn't, he came back and repeated the whole thing. He was getting more and more agitated by the minute.

I stood and decided it was time to go back, even though I had no idea what was bothering him. And just then, I got the creepiest feeling I've ever had. The hair on my neck stood up and I felt like I was being watched. I had to fight the urge to run, because if it were a bear, I knew the last thing one should do is to run. It kicks in their predator instincts.

I had the sense to get Smoky on the leash, as I didn't want him leaving me there alone. If it were something like a bear or mountain lion, I might need his protection.

We had started down the hill when I first heard the sound. I paused, wondering if my ears were playing tricks on me. Sure enough, there it was again. Not too far above me, someone was calling for help. It was fairly faint, but there was no mistake. A distant "Help, help!" was coming from where the aspen were edged by spruce trees, where the forest got thick and dark.

I stopped. Smoky pulled on the leash and wanted badly to keep going, but I made him stay with me. I listened. Surely I was hearing things. Why would anyone be up here, and why would they need help? And if there was someone up here needing help, what could I do to help them?

A shiver went down my spine for no reason. There was nothing to be afraid of, I would just go on down the hill and call the sheriff and tell them what I'd heard. They could come up and help whoever it was. That would be the smart and prudent thing to do.

I felt a sense of relief. I started down the hill again, this time kind of jogging. I needed to hurry back and get someone up here.

But I stopped again. The call was louder and seemed more urgent now.

I didn't want to have someone die because of my fears, but who could be up there? Maybe someone just like me, a hiker from town. But what could be wrong? Maybe they had fallen and broken a leg or something.

I kept this question and answer session going with myself for awhile, trying to decide what to do. Again I heard the cry for help.

I decided to yell back and see what happened. "What's wrong?" I yelled at the top of my lungs.

All I heard back was the same cry for help, "Help, help!" It was kind of spooky, and my intuition said something was wrong, but not something normal.

Now Smoky was pulling hard on the leash, panting, wanting to go home. This confirmed my hunch that something was not right. I decided to run back down the hill and call the sheriff, as I'd wanted to do before. This time, I took off running as fast as I could, Smoky pulling me along. I nearly ate it more than once, going down that steep and hummocky hill.

When we got back into the oak brush, I had to slow down and wind my way through, it was so thick. I had lost the deer trail—I tried pushing my way through the thick scrub, but it was an almost impossible task. That area gets a lot of snow in the winter and enough rain in the summer that the oak brush can have trunks as thick as a person's leg, and trying to push through can be no easy task.

I got through one thicket and came into a small clearing and stopped for a second to catch my breath. I was holding tight onto Smoky's leash, as he was still shaking and trying to get away and run. I was now pretty scared, but not as scared as I had been up above.

Until I heard something to my right, that is, something not that far away.

It sounded like a baby crying.

I stood there for a minute, shocked. What would a baby be doing up here? Did this have something to do with the person calling for help? Had they somehow lost their baby?

My reaction was to go over to the area of the sound and look, but Smoky was now totally panicking. He was a pretty good-sized dog, probably part Collie, and he literally started pulling me down the hill. There was no way I was going to let go of him, no matter what, as he was the only safety margin I had.

I stumbled behind him through the clearing and let him drag me along (not that I had any choice). He was pretty adept at finding holes in the scrub, although sometimes they weren't big enough for me, but I managed to keep pushing through, though the branches and leaves whipped my face and arms, leaving scratches.

We came to another small clearing, and I could now see out enough to gauge where we were. We had somehow steered way off course and were headed more into town, towards Howelsen Hill, the site of the ski jump and alpine slide. My initial thought was to head back towards the subdivision, but I realized I would have to backtrack up a small hill to avoid a big rock outcropping, and there was no way.

We kept going. I decided once we got to the ski hill I would just hike on down it and walk back through town. It was way out of the way, but I didn't care. I just wanted to get to where there were people.

I stopped for a moment again to catch my breath, though Smoky kept pulling. I was breathing hard. Even though it was downhill, jogging and fighting my way through the scrub oak took a lot out of me.

As I stopped, Smoky began growling, but it was different from his normal growl, it was a deep growl like you'd hear from a wolf or wild animal telling you to stay back—an "I mean business" growl. He was such a sweet mellow dog that I was shocked. What was he growling at? He was staring at the bushes to my right.

I tried to see whatever it was that he could see. All I could make out was a black shadow, and it might just be the way the sun was hitting the scrub oak.

But then it moved. I could clearly make out a very large form, at least seven feet tall, and it had shoulders like a football player, but even bigger. Its head came to a bit of a point, but I couldn't make out any features. A very deep terror hit me, the kind that you might feel when fighting for your very survival against some enemy you can't quite see or place.

Once again, Smoky started pulling as hard as he could, trying to get away and run, and I almost lost him. He actually started dragging me so hard I thought I was going to lose my footing. My hand and arm were sore for days afterwards. He pulled me into another thicket, but this time on a deer trail.

We both ran as hard as we could. I was so terrified—I can't explain why, but it was a deep primal fear like our ancestors must have had when being pursued by a dire bear or something like that.

But it didn't make sense. I hadn't even seen enough to even be able to sketch it or anything like that. I wondered if I maybe wasn't letting my fears feed on themselves until I was becoming hysterical. But Smoky's behavior said otherwise. Something was scaring and threatening him. It wasn't just an irrational fear.

Suddenly, I broke through the brush. It was a road! I had come to the road that went to the top of Howelsen Hill. We now started a full-on run as we took off downhill. Within just a minute or so, I came upon some hikers going uphill. I ran past them without even saying hello. Soon, I came to more people, but this group was going downhill. I stopped running and walked behind them a bit. I was exhausted, and hiking down with them would hopefully provide safety in numbers.

I can't tell you how relieved I was. Smoky also settled down. He looked spooked still, but he wasn't shaking anymore and seemed content to just walk along the road.

We got down to the bottom of the hill and walked along the streets back to my sister's house.

She was still at work, as it was mid-afternoon by now. Smoky drank a lot of water, then went and crawled under my sister's bed, where he apparently slept the rest of the afternoon, as he didn't come out until she came back.

When she came home, I told her what had happened. We agreed that I wouldn't be hiking back up there again. We discussed what it could have been, and she asked if maybe we shouldn't call the sheriff. Maybe someone was actually hurt up there.

I decided to err on the side of caution and called the sheriff's office and told them what had happened. They took my number and said they would wait and see if anyone came up missing, as it just wasn't enough evidence to send out a search party. But I knew that no one would come up missing. My intuition and Smoky's actions told me that whatever it was, it wasn't a person, and it wasn't missing.

I left a few days later, still feeling wary and unsettled. I didn't even go anywhere those last few days, except to take Smoky for a few walks around town. I had no desire to be out in the backcountry.

Two weeks to the day after I left, I got a call from my sister. They had decided to move, though it had nothing to do with my experience. They were just really burned out with the winters and cost of living in a ski town.

And had I heard the news? Two hikers had come down off the mountain with a story of something huge stalking them, and it had first made sounds like a crying baby and then starting crying for help. They'd gone to the sheriff and also the press, wanting to make sure people knew about it, as they had actually seen it.

They said it was a Bigfoot.

About the Author
. . . .

Rusty Wilson grew up in the state of Washington, in the heart of Bigfoot country. He didn't know a thing about Bigfoot until he got lost at the age of six and was then found and subsequently adopted by a kindly Bigfoot family.

He lived with them until he was 16, when they finally gave up on ever socializing him into Bigfoot ways (he hated garlic and pancakes, refused to sleep in a nest, wouldn't hunt wild pigs, and on top of it all, his feet were small).

His Bigfoot family then sent him off to Evergreen State College in nearby Olympia, thinking it would be liberal enough to take care of a kid with few redeeming qualities, plus they liked the thick foliage around the college and figured Rusty could live there, saving them money for housing.

At Evergreen, Rusty studied wildlife biology, eventually returning to the wilds, after first learning to read and write and regale everyone with his wild tales. He eventually became a flyfishing guide, and during his many travels in the wilds, he collected stories from others who have had contact with Bigfoot, also known as Sasquatch.

Because of his background, Rusty is considered to be the world's foremost Bigfoot expert (at least so by himself, if not by anyone else). He's spent many a fun evening around campfires with his clients, telling stories. Some of those clients had some pretty good stories of their own.

If you've enjoyed this, you might want to read *Rusty Wilson's Bigfoot Campfire Stories,* as well as *Rusty Wilson's More Bigfoot Campfire Stories,* available as ebooks at yellowcatbooks.com, amazon.com, and bn.com. They are also available in print at Amazon.com.

You can follow and communicate with Rusty at his blog at rustybigfoot.blogspot.com. And check out the Bigfoot Headquarters at yellowcatbooks.com.

And if you enjoyed this book, you will also like *The Ghost Rock Cafe,* a Bigfoot mystery by Chinle Miller. Also available at yellowcatbooks.com, bn.com, and Amazon. com.

Whether you're a Bigfoot believer or not, we hope you enjoyed these tall tales...or are they really true stories?

Only Rusty and his fellow storytellers know for sure.

13275339R00138

Made in the USA
Lexington, KY
25 January 2012